A Warr   eart
The Awakening

A Warrior's Heart
The Awakening

L. Neil Thrussell

Best U Can B Inc.

Published by *Best U Can B Inc.*
www.bestucanb.ca

ISBN 978-0-9739042-4-6

Cover Art: Lyle Schultz, *ProMedia Solutions*
Editing: Tracy Blaine, *The Write Support*

"This delightful and compelling story about a man's desire for a deeper existence is entertaining and enlightening. *A Warrior's Heart: The Awakening* shares a transformation we all long for - how to become a more conscious, heart-centered being. Through the journey, you'll be inspired to take a different look at how you live your own life."
- *Shawne Duperon,* Six-Time EMMY® Winner, ShawneTV.

"LOVE this book! A wonderful adventure of survival and self-exploration, it's a brilliant, engaging read from start to finish. You will not want to put it down."
- *Teresa de Grosbois,* Word Of Mouth Marketing Expert, Bestselling Author, International Speaker, Founder of The Evolutionary Business Council.

"What a delightful tale of self-discovery, friendship, the power of love and a journey of awakening to spirituality!"
- *Marilyn Suttle,* Coauthor of the bestseller *Who's Your Gladys?* and creator of *the Suttle Shift*

"Places for living and learning are sacred; some more so than others. When Graham interacts with Master Akio during his reflective journey on the island, every place of Akio's unfolding story is important. The more Graham learns, the more Akio's story enfolds into Graham. Then comes the amazing point in their friendship when Graham has a knowing; he knows how much sand becomes a sand pile, then a sand dune, without counting each grain of sand. This awareness was Master Aiko's miraculous gift to Graham."
- *Stephen Hobbs,* EdD, Master Navigator, Wellthy=Wealthy Entrepreneur Program, WELLth Learning.com

"What I love about Neil is his down home practical approach to life, love, and freedom. No *New Age* non-sense in this man! His book is a great read, one I know you will enjoy!"
- *Stephen Garrett,* Author, Coach and Speaker

"*A Warrior's Heart: The Awakening* conveys that there is a divine plan for each one of us. The Awakening lies in the heart of every person, and their life journey illuminates the path. Open your heart to love and live your life in harmony with the world around us."
- **Svetlana Kim,** Bestselling Author of *White Pearl and I: A Memoir of a Political Refugee* and Spokesperson for the 2011 Macy's Asian Pacific American Heritage Month

"I've never read a spiritual story before, so I wasn't sure if I'd like this. On the evening that I read the last page of the book, I declared, "There'd better be a sequel to this! I want to know what happens to Graham after this!" That same night I dreamed about Akio. I miss both these guys - hurry up and finish that second book!"
- **Colleen Bartsch**, Caterer and Farmer's Wife

"Hang on to your seat! You're in for one heck of an adventure! *A Warrior's Heart: The Awakening* is an Indiana Jones-style adventure that transforms you along the way. It is a wonderfully captivating journey to the edge and beyond... for the characters in the book and for YOU. This story will entertain you, have you asking questions that you haven't asked before, and make an adventurer out of you. Your Warrior spirit will grow and your Heart will be touched deeply!"
- **Satyen Raja,** Trainer, Author, Chief Passion Igniter at Ignite Passion Now

"You will discover in *A Warrior's Heart: The Awakening,* the greatest adventure is the spiritual quest to awaken to the truth that you always have been, and always will be, loveable and loved. You will learn that it is through finding a place of stillness within and letting go of how you think things should be, or should have been, that you can truly open to love and discover the extraordinary in the everyday ordinary tasks of living."
- **Jacqueline Bignell**, Executive Producer, The Difference Movie

"*A Warrior's Heart: The Awakening* is a delightful story of enlightenment and awakening! As each chapter of this man's story unfolded, I found myself being caught up in curiosity about what was going to happen next.

Many would consider me a junkie of personal growth materials and study resources. I'm fascinated by the wealth of personal development and spiritual growth books that are so readily available at our finger tips these days.

A Warrior's Heart: The Awakening was one of my favorite reads this year.

I thoroughly enjoyed experiencing the transformation of the hardcore, tough edged, bad ass pilot (out of shape mentally, physically, and emotionally), who returns to the site of a plane crash that he was responsible for (through his own arrogance) to discover himself.

The Universe grants him a masterful teacher and he quickly comes to discover that reveling in his emotional pain and suffering has to become a thing of the past. He realizes that he is a willing and – eventually - gracious student experiencing the journey of a lifetime…his lifetime. He faces many changes over the course of the next 30 days, in ways that he'd never imagined.

This story kept me captivated and curious about the next lesson Graham would experience in his daily adventures. The moments of his bliss became the moments of my bliss as I experienced the expression of his heart expanding and growing.

This book is a story that I truly enjoyed reading. I loved the deeper message that continually built as building blocks for the foundation of true spiritual awakening: the bigger our heart, the greater our understanding and greater our capacity to touch another person's life.

A Warrior's Heart: The Awakening certainly has touched a place in my heart, reaffirming the greatest gifts in our life come from connection to our Source and not our pain. A must read!"
- **Nancy Battye,** *Speaker, Writer, Radio Show & Interview Host, Life Coach*

"*A Warrior's Heart: The Awakening* is a book which invites you to use all your senses when you read it. In so many ways, this book is a great expression of taking time for yourself, listening to the voices within. The learning is presented in a powerful way, inviting you to be part of the day to day experiences journeying along with what could be part of the awakening process."

- ***Sheila Unique***, Best-selling author of *Quick Shifts*

Acknowledgements

As with any major undertaking or endeavor, one does not succeed without a fantastic support team behind them, and this book is no different. Since this is my first published work, I really don't want to forget anyone that helped me along the way in the creation and/or production of this book.

First off, a special thank you to Anna-Mae Fipke, you showed me that with some loving editing I actually could write... Thank you.

A big thank you to Lyle Schultz, who appeared to have read my mind and produced the perfect book cover for me on the first try! Thank you, Lyle!

Thank you to:

My Hapkido instructor and friend, Bobby Triantafillou, (Fifth Dan) who gave me an introduction to Kendo - The Way of The Sword;

My manuscript proofing team: Tim Summers, Allan and Colleen Bartsch, Julie Friedman-Smith, Anaya Lea. This book is a testament to your dedication to this project. Thank you all!;

Tracy Blaine of *The Write Support* whose final edits brought life and depth to the story;

Susanne Lampier for her skills in formatting this book;

My friend, Adam Hunt, who talked me through crashing a plane, without loss of life!

I send a special shout of thanks to all my friends at the *Evolutionary Business Council*. Thank you for your support.

I extend thanks to my family:

To my Mom, Jean, who instilled the dreamer deep within me, along with a belief that anything is possible. To my Dad, Doug, who taught me how to create, fix and build almost anything with my hands (especially boats as a small child – inside family joke). To my sisters, Glenda and Sherry, and my brother, Douglas, who taught me to stand up for myself and for showing me what family was really about, and who, to this day, continually remind me that I had an exceptionally great childhood. I have so many fond, fun and silly memories with them. Thanks! Love you all.

To Tina's Dad, Roger, and Step-mom, Mary-Lou, who have taught me that no matter how hard you get knocked down, you just dust yourself off, take a deep breath and then start all over again. To Tina's Mom, Mickey, who continually keeps on showing me that age is just a number and you need to always have fun. Hmmm, Tina's sister, Lori - Master Akio has a little bit of Lori in him, with his willingness to try. There is always someone in every group that teaches you to dance to the beat of your own drum, and that would be my brother in-law, Nigel. To Wray, Harold and Gina, Master Akio has a little bit of all of you in him, with his willingness to adapt, learn and accept. Thank you all!

To all of my eleven nephews and nieces, you have taught me to stay young. You have taught me to love in so many different ways. I have enjoyed every moment we have spent together (and I wish your parents would have stopped feeding you all so you wouldn't have grown up so fast!) Michael, Andrew, Paul, Sandya, Daniel, Amanda, Thomas, Landon, Samantha, Robin and Olivia - You are all loved.

Dedication

How do I adequately thank the love of my life for being there on the journey with me for all these many, many years? The one who encouraged me right from the first moment I said, "I had this dream and I would like to write a novel." The one who spent hours pouring over my manuscript and doing an initial edit, despite my crazy use of commas, and has continued to encourage me to keep writing.

By dedicating *A Warrior's Heart: The Awakening* to her.

I love you more than I am able to put into words, Tina . . . Know this, Master Akio's love and tenderness comes from you. Thank you.

With love and devotion I dedicate this book to Tina Thrussell, my friend, my lover, my wife.

In Love and Light,

L. Neil Thrussell

Table of Contents

The Adventure Begins

I heard and felt the plane shake as the second engine on the Lear jet 60 quit. Just fucking great! We're out of fuel in the middle of the Pacific Ocean! Just great! I heard the ram air turbine drop into place. "Well, at least we still have hydraulics," I said to Blaine, my co-pilot of almost four years. "Yes, at least that's one good thing," he replied nervously.

Blaine reached up and switched off the engine warning alarm; the giant Nag, as I like to call it. The temperature in the cockpit hadn't changed in the last few moments, but I could feel beads of sweat roll down the side of my ribs. The yoke was already slippery from my perspiring hands. I was definitely scared.

Blaine stretched over and behind me to grab my oxygen mask. I could see the fear written in his eyes as he handed it to me. In turn, I reached behind Blaine and passed him his mask. I tried to hide my growing panic, but I'm sure he could see it clearly, despite my efforts.

I quickly placed the oxygen mask over my face and rapidly adjusted the straps. I pushed the test button to verify I had oxygen. I heard a Phhhhssst sound escape from the mask's regulator. I checked to make sure the positive oxygen flow light was on. I grabbed the microphone jack cord that was attached to my mask and plugged it into the electronics console. Then I turned to make sure Blaine had his mask on. He gave me the thumbs up. I confirmed that his positive oxygen flow light was on, as well.

My thoughts were swimming. How the hell did this happen? How did we run out fuel? I know I calculated it correctly. I don't make those types of mistakes. The idiots that filled us up must not have put in enough fuel!

I reached over to switch on the radio and stole a worried glance towards Blaine. "Mayday, mayday, mayday, this is Charlie Foxtrot Alpha Bravo Charlie. We are five eight five nautical miles North, Northeast of Majuro at flight level one two five. Double engine failure, ditching, two souls-on-board, over.

I waited for fifteen or twenty seconds – it felt like an eternity - then switched the radio to 121.5 MHz. Majuro tower hadn't answered but maybe another aircraft in the area would. "Mayday, mayday, mayday, this is Charlie Foxtrot Alpha Bravo Charlie. We are five eight five nautical miles North, Northeast of Majuro at flight level one two five. Double engine failure, ditching, two souls-on-board, over.

The silence was excruciating; I was too scared to say anything. Besides, I didn't know what to say. The only thing I could hear was my panicked breaths in the oxygen mask and the sound of my heart pounding in my ears. A plane was not supposed to be this quiet.

I switched on the radio again, "Mayday, mayday, mayday, this is Charlie Foxtrot Alpha Bravo Charlie. We are five eight five nautical miles North, Northeast of Majuro at flight level one two five. Double engine failure, ditching, two souls-on-board, over.

Again nothing!

****

I felt horribly dizzy. Waves of nausea twisted and wracked my body. I was in agony. I stumbled to the edge of the palm trees and wretched my lunch. As I wiped my mouth with my hand, I slipped into full scale panic - just as before. It was the same feeling of abandonment I had experienced the last time I was here on the island, just after the plane crash. It was all too familiar and just as terrifying.

My mind frantically raced in every direction, thoughts jumping randomly until one clear and concise idea blasted through my frenzied, fogged-in mind. This time it was my choice to be here. This time I had put myself here. *Graham, what the hell are you doing?*

I looked up and watched Captain Taka and the Nanami pull away. My stomach lurched and my head started to pound. I ran wildly to the water's edge, screaming hysterically, "Wait! Come back! I've changed my mind!" Waving my arms wildly in the air, desperately jumping up and down, I screamed, "Come back! Come back! Don't leave me here!"

I saw Captain Taka turn to look at me. I waved harder, motioning for him to turn his boat around and come back. He simply raised his hand, gave me a friendly wave back, and churned off into the vastness of the open ocean.

I stared in disbelief as the Nanami and its captain become a small dot on the horizon. Absolute terror raced through my body as the enormity of my reckless decision came crashing down upon me. My legs buckled beneath me. My face ploughed into the hot sand. I began to shake uncontrollably. *Graham, what have you done?*

My brain raced wildly, seized by the fact that I was now totally alone on a deserted island. Again. I was stuck in the middle of nowhere with no TV, no internet, no pizza delivery, no nothing! Alone, abandoned, 24/7 – for 30 days! Not the three days I was marooned here last time. *30 days! Shit! What was I thinking?*

Graham Alexander Connelly, my mind screeched vehemently, *camping, to you, is a five-star hotel; roughing it is anything less than that! What on earth are you doing here?* The question broke my panic just enough to allow for the realization that, this time, I could phone Captain Taka at any time and request that he come and pick me up. Even though he did not respond to my frantic waving, I somehow knew he would come back if I called him.

With that understanding, the fear slowly began to subside. My heart beat began to slow. I eased myself to a sitting position and the pain in my chest began to lessen. I stared long and hard at the open, relentless ocean, but could no longer see any sign of the Nanami. *Okay, now what?*

I became aware of the sand that now caked my face. It was in my ears and my nose. My teeth were gritty and my mouth was as dry as a desert. "Get up," I said. No one could hear me, so what did it matter if I chastized myself? "Get your fat, lazy, out-of-shape body into the water and clean up. Quit wallowing in self-pity. You put yourself here!"

I decided to go look for my swimsuit. As I struggled to stand, I was struck by a wave of amusement. How absurd! Here I was, master and ruler of my own deserted island, and I was going to don a swimsuit. "Wow!" I said, as I realized I was so conditioned to wear a swimsuit that I never considered NOT packing one. I wondered how many other things I did without thinking.

I left my sand-caked clothes on the beach and walked into the warm, tropical water. As I lazily floated in the salt water I couldn't help but notice that the jungle was really thick behind the area I intended to set up as home for the next month. It was dense with palm trees, tall grasses and a bunch of trees that I couldn't identify; I hadn't thought about researching trees and vegetation when I was preparing for my stay on the island. I'm not a colors kind of guy, but the jungle seemed to be painted in hundreds of different shades of green. I just noticed

5

this for the first time, which was weird because I'd been on this island before.

Hours later, after I had unpacked most of my belongings and set up camp, I gently and gingerly laid down on my cot. I was curiously pleased with myself. Setting up and organizing the tent went well, although it would have been a lot better if I hadn't stayed out so long in the sun without sunscreen. Thank goodness it was just my shoulders and back that were burned.

I'd wrapped a tarp over my gear for the night because I was too tired and too burned to string up an awning as I'd originally planned. I decided I would finish setting up my camp in the morning – or whenever I could move my shoulders again.

I looked at my watch and let out a pathetic little whimper. "Man, it's only six o'clock! It's already dark out and I'm already in bed. This could be a long 30 days!" I was too worn out to do anything but sleep.

Day One

It seemed only minutes had passed when I woke up. I let out a groan as I sleepily looked at my watch. It was 6:13 a.m. My shoulders still hurt, and my tent was already becoming unbearably hot.

I gently inched my way to an upright position and painfully reached for the sunscreen. To the best of my limited abilities, I applied a very liberal amount to whatever parts of my body I could reach. I then rummaged through my clothes for a shirt and a pair of shorts. I begrudgingly slipped on my sandals and headed out of my already sweltering tent.

As I turned to zip-up the tent, I selfishly smiled. Back home people were at work while I was camping on a sandy beach surrounded by palm trees, overlooking a crystal blue ocean. *My life is good; even with a wicked sun burn.*

It hit me that this was probably the first time I'd ever thought my life was actually good. I'd pretty much decided long ago that it sucked.

I walked over to one of my many coolers for a cold bottle of water. I twisted off the cap and drank deeply. "Ah!" Plain water never tasted so good. I could hardly wait until tonight for one of the three dozen cold beers I brought with me.

I looked around until I spied my folding chair. I set it up under the shade of a palm tree and sat down rather cautiously and delicately. "I'll be glad when this sunburn is healed," I said to myself.

I took a drink of water and settled in to experience the true beauty and splendor of my very first morning in paradise. I realized I was still smiling. I raised my water bottle in a toast to honour the ocean, "To a good life!" and took another big swallow of water. I sat looking directly over the cove and out into the sparkling blue ocean in utter amazement and awe.

As I lazily gazed upon the waters, I had to admit I was feeling rather odd, almost out of sorts. In all my 42 years, I couldn't remember ever feeling anything quite like this. The quote from the going away card that Sara, my boss, gave me just prior to boarding my flight for this crazy adventure, jumped into my head:

"Many men die at twenty-five and aren't buried until they are seventy-five." - Benjamin Franklin

I didn't understand at first, but now I realized that Sara was hinting I wasn't really living my life. I chuckled to myself, "Isn't sitting on a folding chair, in the middle of the Pacific Ocean, all by myself, really living?"

My chair squeaked beneath me as I wrestled my tender, sunburned body out and moved slowly towards my supplies. "Some breakfast is in order," I said to myself, "before I spend the whole day in some weird, melancholic funk."

By the end of the day, despite my increasingly painful sunburn, I had managed to get a lot of things done. I set up my latrine area; set up the cooking area; restacked my supplies; and even managed to gather firewood for the evening. The only things I didn't get done were to hang my awning over the cooking area and explore more of the island. I was extremely proud of myself. *Job well done, Graham! Hopefully, you'll be able to do that tomorrow, too.*

I stood back on the beach admiring my handy work. I had done a pretty good job creating my new 'home'. Not bad for a guy who traditionally camped at five-star hotels. Thank God for Google and Sara! I would have been completely lost without their help getting me organized and making sure I had the right camping equipment. Mind you, six weeks ago I would never have thought I'd be here again.

I smiled. I may have fantasized about being stranded on a deserted island in my youth, but my fantasies usually included a bevy of naked women with me. I certainly didn't have my dream companions here. I also wasn't really in the middle of the ocean. I was actually about 180 miles east of Wotje Atoll. This was part of the Marshall Islands, approximately 3,000 miles east of the Philippines and 2,000 miles northeast of Papua New Guinea. Hawaii is technically more in the middle of the Pacific Ocean than the Marshall Islands.

I had to sit down. I hadn't really thought about my plane crash since arriving yesterday, but thinking about Hawaii brought all the excruciatingly, dumb, arrogant, stupid, idiotic, selfish, asinine, and completely crazy details back to me. The chair creaked as I dropped into it. I didn't even notice the discomfort of my sunburned shoulders as I slumped against the back of the chair.

It really was to be a simple, routine flight. We - my co-pilot, Blaine, and I - were asked to fly a Learjet 60 from Honolulu, Hawaii to Port Moresby, Papua New Guinea. The company we both worked for had purchased a new jet for their executive fleet and had sold the Learjet we were flying to a company in Port Moresby. Blaine and I had flown that plane together many times before.

When we took off we knew we were going to skirt the outside edges of a thunderstorm as we approached Majuro Atoll in the Marshall Islands. I was counting on making a refueling stop there. What I didn't count on was how lazy I had become as a captain. I was taking us over dangerous territory - vast amounts of open water - and I didn't even bother to check, let alone recheck, my fuel calculations. Poor Blaine was so used to me yelling at him for no apparent reason that he didn't risk asking to check my fuel calculations, even though it was part of his job as co-pilot. And because my sloppy calculations went unchecked we didn't make it to Majuro Atoll.

It was more than a little sobering to admit that because of my miserable, cocky, arrogance I had very casually placed the life of my co-pilot and friend in danger.

My friend. It's funny that it wasn't until we were stranded on this island that I realized Blaine was my friend and not just my co-pilot. For those three terrifying days, Blaine never once brought up the fact that it was my fault we were forced to ditch our plane into the Pacific. He never got mad at me for my lack of basic survival skills and he always talked about what we were going to do when we got off the island. He talked about us getting together in a couple weeks to have a Bar-B-Q at his place. He talked about us flying together again.

Looking out over the ocean I reflected on the whole situation. *What kind of friend am I?*

I immediately felt like I'd been sucker punched in my stomach. If it wasn't for Blaine and Sara, I would have no friends at all. I had pretty much driven everyone else away. I was so caught up in my own personal self-pity I couldn't see anyone or anything but my own miserable life. With a body-wracking sob I cried out loud, "I could have killed him!"

The pain of my revelation intensified as I realized that besides almost killing one of my only friends, I would have taken away the daddy of two of the sweetest little girls in the whole wide world. My body twisted with remorse and grief. In between spasms, I somehow managed to sorrowfully whimper, "I'm sorry, Blaine." And for the first time in my pitiful life I meant it. I was truly sorry for my actions. I felt remorse for what I had done to another person.

I don't know how long I cried, or was doubled over in grief, but ever so slowly, I became aware of the gradual shifting of the light. I was gently drawn out of my remorse and into the beautiful sunset in my front yard. The colours were more intense and vibrant than any I had seen before. Breathtaking hues of red and orange spread before me. I was awestruck. I laughed at myself. I'd seen hundreds, maybe thousands of sunsets. My mind told me I was being silly, but the beautiful sight shut down my mind. Silly or not, I was absolutely mesmerized by the sheer splendor before me.

I inhaled a deep, full breath. Slowly I pushed down on the arms of my chair. Painfully, my shoulders responded and lifted my aching body. I stood on the beach drinking in the magnificent scene. Without taking my eyes off the sunset, I slipped out of my clothes and let them fall to the sand and waded into the warm, soothing, tropical water.

Day Two

I awoke with a start; the tent was starting to get warm. I glanced at my watch. It was 5:30 am. Soon the sun would be up fully and my tent would be an unbearable sauna, but I was extremely reluctant to get out of bed. I was feeling content and happy, and I wasn't ready to let go of those feelings yet. I chuckled to myself, "Graham, you're getting soft." I couldn't remember feeling like this before.

I fell asleep last night replaying the sunset in my mind. Vividly recalling these images now, it was easy to lose myself in that sense of awe and wonder again. The ever increasing heat in my tent brought me back to the present. Cautiously, attempting not to aggravate my sunburn, I swung my legs out of the cot. I slowly raised myself to a standing position. "So far so good," I said. Gingerly, I raised my arms parallel to my shoulders. *Still tender, but I'm pretty sure I can set up the awning today.*

The temperature inside the tent was increasing rapidly. I didn't want to take much longer to get myself ready to face my day. I dressed in the clothes from the previous day and carefully exited the tent.

Standing just outside, I wondered aloud, "So what should I do now?" I excitedly remembered that Sara said she left me a package in one of my dry goods containers. I smiled as I murmured, "Well, Graham, you have something to do now."

It took me about ten minutes to sort through the containers before I found Sara's carefully wrapped package. I put the lids back on and rewrapped all of the containers in the tarp. I proceeded to grab a bottle of water and my chair, and took Sara's package to what was quickly becoming my favourite location on the beach.

I settled quickly into my chair and was about to rip into Sara's package when I realized I hadn't looked at my exquisite kingdom today. I lifted my head and scanned over the island and out to the ocean. Once again, I had to smile. I was here while the rest of the world was at work.

I wondered if I could actually buy this island. It's wasn't on any of the official charts. My interpreter really had to work hard to convince Captain Taka that an island actually existed at this location.

As I sat in my chair, I decided that today was the day I would explore. I liked that my biggest decision for the day would be whether to go right or left from camp - my home. I continued to smile as I looked out over the crystal blue water.

I felt the weight of Sara's present resting in my lap. I picked up the present and studied it. My first observation was that Sara was a meticulous wrapper; all the creases and edges were straight and crisp. Sara used very little tape. Not like me, who thought it was fun to finish wrapping presents with a whole roll of clear packing tape. Anyone who got a present from me had to use a knife to get into it. I gently peeled the tape from one of the carefully creased edges, unfolded every one, and peeled off the last bit of tape before I lifted the wrapping paper to reveal the gift. I saw an envelope delicately taped to a book. With care, I unfastened the envelope, slid out the card, and opened it to reveal a beautifully handwritten note.

Dear Graham,

I trust you are enjoying your much needed time alone. I always thought you to be a 'cold beer and lots of scantily clad girls on a deserted island' type of guy. ☺ But it appears we can always surprise ourselves and others with our actions. I hope you enjoy the beer.

I don't know when you will find this, but I trust it will be at the right time, whenever that is. Graham, this journal is not to be used as fire starter; it is to be used as a way to record your thoughts, feelings, and experiences while on your island.

I suggest you allow your thoughts to flow onto the page without editing. It doesn't matter if you think a thought is dumb. Write down it anyway.

> Graham, a lot of highly
> successful people journal, so
> please don't wrinkle your nose
> and make fun of it. Just give it a
> try.

I had to smile. Sara knew me way too well. I felt my face begin to relax; I'd been wrinkling my nose at the thought of journaling.

> Graham, this journal, including
> the cover and art work, was
> handmade in Africa. The inside
> pages are a fine linen. This is a
> representation of fine quality. It
> is symbolic: If you are going to
> do something, make sure you do
> it well, or don't do it at all.
>
> I look forward to hearing stories
> of your adventures upon your
> return.
>
> Graham, I leave you with this
> quote:
>
> "Be yourself; everyone else is
> already taken." ~ Oscar Wilde
>
> Respectfully,
> Sara
>
> P.S. Normally, I end my letters
> and notes to friends with "In
> Love and Light," but I'm really
> not sure how you would take
> that.

There appeared to be a lot in this note; I knew I was getting some of it, but in truth, I did not entirely understand. I had a vague notion of what love was, but I didn't have the foggiest idea what this "Light" thing was all about, or her comment, "but I trust it will be at the right time, whenever that is."

I picked up the journal and carefully examined the outside artwork. It must have taken the artist hours to make the cover. *Man, I could never do this. I don't have the patience for something like this.*

With care, I opened the front cover. The pages inside were crisp and slightly off-white in colour. The page was smooth and soft. Inside the front cover there was a small sticky note. It simply said, "When you're ready to write, there's a special pen waiting for you inside the beer cooler."

I decided I'd wait to go find the 'special' pen. Actually, I wasn't sure I'd ever be ready to do something stupid like journaling. I appreciated the gift, just not the idea of spilling my guts on paper.

I got up from my chair, walked over to the tent, and carefully placed my new journal on the cot inside. I may not understand the journaling idea, but I knew Sara went to a lot of effort and expense for that book, so I wasn't going to wreck it. I at least owed her the honour of respecting the present.

That thought caught me entirely off guard. Since when did I start caring about other people's feelings? *Shit! This island is doing weird things to me! I think the heat is making me soft. The next thing you know, I'll want to sit around a group campfire, roast marshmallows, and sing songs like Kumbaya!* That thought made me shudder. I made fun of idiots who did the 'sing songs at group campfires' scene.

As I stood in the middle of the tropical sauna otherwise known as my tent, a sudden chorus of growls broke the silence and reminded me that I hadn't had breakfast. I was starving. Apparently my stomach wanted breakfast to be my next plan of action for the day! Stepping out of the tent and zipping it closed, I muttered, "Breakfast it is."

I looked down at my wrist and saw my watch. I chuckled. I don't have any place to be at any particular time. *I'll eat when I'm hungry.* I unclasped my watch and placed it with my clothes. It was weird. The simple act of taking off my watch made me feel lighter. It was like some invisible weight had been lifted. I exited the tent and headed to the kitchen area.

There was one thing I was absolutely sure of; I was NOT going to starve on this island. I made sure I brought enough food to fuel my portly body (and possibly an entire village if they happened to come by) for this thirty day adventure. I love food, which could be why my doctor continually inserted the word DIET into my yearly checkups over the last ten years.

But, first things first. Even though it was probably 80° Fahrenheit already, I still loved and needed my morning cup of coffee.

It wasn't long before I had the coffee prepared and percolating on the propane stove. My next task was to cut up potatoes and onions for some good old-fashioned chunky fried spuds. *Mmm... I love the smell of fried food!*

In short order I had a small mountain of potatoes chopped. I was blissfully dicing up a few onions when the coffee pot erupted all over the stove. I quickly reached over and turned off the stove. After cleaning up the mess, I eagerly grabbed my coffee cup and poured myself some steaming, black gold. With cup in hand, I turned and faced the ocean. "Cheers!" I raised my cup to the horizon and took a cautious sip. Absolute bliss.

With a loud, hollow rumble my stomach reminded me of the next order of business. I grabbed some eggs and a couple slices of bacon out of the cooler. I was ready.

After a few minutes of mixing and frying, my gastronomic concoction was ready. I scooped out a gigantic mass of my sumptuous all-in-one-pan fried breakfast, refilled my coffee cup and hurried to my chair to enjoy the view with my meal. I quickly settled into my chair, piled a huge mound of potatoes onto my fork, and let out a loud groan of appreciation with the first mouthful. This was a well cooked meal! "Mmm... this is so good!" I exclaimed.

I finished off my initial plateful and helped myself to another plate-load of bliss. *This one is for dessert!* Besides, I couldn't let all this great food go to waste! I smiled at my own cleverness.

I managed to down the whole pot of coffee while admiring the sheer beauty of the ocean and the cove. As I gazed out into the vast expanse of the ocean, I noticed high forming cumulonimbus clouds on the horizon. *The weather is changing. It's going to rain soon.* It was time to put my awning up or I wouldn't have a place to cook or eat soon.

I forced myself to get up and took my dishes to the kitchen area. Grudgingly, I started heating the dishwater on the stove. To be efficient, I went looking for all the materials I would need to set up the awning while the water warmed.

Soon the dishwashing and drying were complete and everything was put away. It was now time to get that awning up. I was not looking forward to this part.

It took a lot of swearing, sweating, and a huge amount of strenuous physical effort to get the four corner ropes up the trees. My portly forty-two-year-old body was really not meant to scale palm trees (or any tree, for that matter). When I finally had the ropes up, all I had left to do was attach the awning to the ropes, and haul it up. But by now I was just too exhausted to do it. Between the heat of the day, my sunburn, and being really out of shape, I had nothing left in me. I grabbed a bottle of water and returned to my chair. My refuge. My sanctuary.

God, Graham, you are really out of shape! I slumped in my chair, feeling in a rather foul mood. I had secretly dreaded putting up the stupid awning. I knew I was so badly out of shape that I would struggle with the whole darn setup procedure, but I wasn't willing to admit it.

It really pissed me off that Blaine and Sara were right to question my choice of awnings. They wanted me to buy a free-standing one; something that came right out of a box, with poles and no prerequisite or special skills needed for assembly or construction; an awning that was easily staked into the ground. They didn't want me to buy one that would require climbing trees, physical strength or dexterity, but I insisted I could handle it.

I really hated it when others were right about my limited talents or skills. I knew that I was out of shape, but I bloody well didn't want to admit to it. Now, after climbing the trees and physically hauling on ropes, I had no place to hide. I had to admit to myself how pathetically weak I had become.

A stupid little smirk spread over my face. "Round is a great shape," I chuckled to myself. Well, I may be round, but at least I still had my sense of humour.

I groaned as I slowly rose out of my chair. *I might as well finish the job, even if it kills me.*

I spent the next half hour tightening and retightening ropes to get the awning just right. Now the kitchen / dining room had a roof and I had a place to sit and keep dry when it rained. There was no IF regarding rain in this part of the Pacific. It was just a matter of how much, how long, and how hard.

I was relatively exhausted by this time. I barely managed to wobble to the fine sandy beach that was now my front yard. I began scanning the horizon. It would probably rain tonight or later that afternoon. There was not a ship in sight, or any indication of activity on the vast waters. I was truly alone in the near middle of nowhere. My heart skipped a few beats at the thought, but I didn't have a panic attack like when Captain Taka left me on the island yesterday. None the less, I was still uncomfortable with the idea of being alone.

Childishly, I decided I need a name for MY island. *Graham, what do you want call your island? What do you want to call this magnificent cove in front of you?* My mind drew a blank. I'd never had the opportunity to name something before. I never had any pets as a child, all my friends came with their own names, and the planes I'd flown also already had names. This was an entirely new experience for me.

I could call the cove something like 'Crystal Blue Water Cove' or 'Connelly's Cove' after myself or … I could call it 'Sara's Cove.' I had no idea why Sara's name popped into my head, but as soon it did, no other came to mind. The cove just had to be 'Sara's Cove', in honour of the one person who really supported me going on this adventure from the very start.

In my most noble and regal voice, I declared, "This cove shall forever be known as Sara's Cove." It felt childish, and yet it felt right making this indulgent proclamation. It felt especially fitting to say it out loud.

I have the name of the cove, but what should I call the island? I paused and reflected for a moment, but nothing came to me. "I guess the water gods are NOT ready to let me know," I muttered. *Water gods?* I shook my head in disbelief. *Graham, you're going soft in the head!*

I decided to do lunch before I completely lost it. I turned and walked up the beach towards my kitchen to prepare a feast fit for a king. King Graham, to be exact!

As I stood in front of the coolers, my brain seemed to turn off. I couldn't think of what to make for lunch. I had just eaten a short while ago, so I wasn't really all that hungry, but I was convinced I should eat something. Then it hit me. Lunch was going to be nut trail mix and fruit bars. I was going to go on an adventure and explore more of the island. I got excited at the thought of my upcoming quest. I was going to see parts of the island that, quite possibly, had never been seen before. *That's very cool!*

I slathered on more sunscreen, grabbed my hat, and two bottles of water. Then I just stood there. Should I go left or right?

I thought my plane crash site was off to the left, but it had already been a rough day. *Do I really want to face any more of my demons today? Am I genuinely prepared to retrace my steps?*

I was immediately lost in the memory of walking across a series of tiny islands connected by sand bars. There were maybe eight or ten separate islands. Most of the sand bars were easy to walk across, but a few had deeper water between them, where I had to swim about 200 yards. I really struggled with that journey.

Look at me. What am I thinking? I wasn't exactly alone on that journey. Blaine was with me on that walk along the outer islands. Blaine and I both had to wade or swim in between the smaller islands. It was Blaine and I that crashed into the ocean. It was Blaine and I that were marooned on the deserted island. It was Blaine and I that were rescued three days after the crash. It was Blaine and I that lived through this together.

And it was Blaine that had a huge group of people meet him at the airport in Honolulu. It was Blaine who had a wife and kids to greet him. Me? If it wasn't for Sara, I would have had no one to greet me.

If I hadn't been responsible for crashing the plane and almost getting us killed; if I'd had someone at the airport to greet me on my safe arrival, I don't think I would be doing this. I don't think I would be alone on this island in the near middle of the Pacific Ocean.

Hmmm, I wonder if this is what Sara meant by, "There are no accidents in life, only learning opportunities?"

I came back to the present moment and, for no other reason than to appear brave in my own mind, I chose to go left. Or so I told myself. The truth was I didn't feel like I had a choice; I was absolutely compelled to go left. I felt like there was an outside force or energy guiding me along.

Yet to even consider that there was a force beyond me was pretty weird for me. If I was to admit this potential, unseen energy was a possibility, I would also have to consider the possibility that I was put on this planet for a reason. It would mean there was a reason for my wretched childhood. It would mean there could be more to life than enjoying beer and watching sports.

Shaking off this deep thinking, I turned left and, with water bottles in hand, began walking along the beach. I thought I'd see if I could circumnavigate the island first. I'd look for any interesting sights and mark the way points in my GPS. GPS! Crap! I did an abrupt about-face and went directly to my tent. I found myself grumbling as I searched for my GPS in my bags. "Graham, you idiot! It's too hot in here to be forgetting things in the tent. Don't do this again!"

I finally found my GPS and switched it on. It had full power; it was working. At last, I was ready to go. I closed the bags and exited the tent, zipping it closed behind me. I was happy to be out of the sweltering heat trap.

I headed over to my favourite spot and sat in my chair to punch a few buttons on the GPS. As my starting reference I typed in, 'My Living Room'. I smiled at the thought of this splendid spot being MY living room.

Going left along the beach, I punched in numerous way points as I walked. 'Big jutting rock, giant palm tree leaning towards ocean.' It was disappointing to find nothing of real significance. No volcanoes, no caves, not even whales on the horizon. Just ominous rain clouds.

I had walked for close to twenty minutes when I decided it was time to turn around and look back to see what I could see of 'My Home'. I was startled to see how far I had come. I could just barely make out the kitchen, bedroom, and living room.

I turned again and looked back up the beach in the direction I had been walking. It appeared that the landscape took a sharp turn to the left about 50 yards in front of me. Curious, I carried on. Here, the island landscape did indeed turn left. It was such a deep bend that as soon as I had walked around it I could no longer see my home. I entered the way point and description in the GPS as 'Dog Leg'. I continued walking along the beach entering more way points and descriptions as I went.

I was startled by the lone cry of a sea gull. The gull was lazily soaring high above me, heading in-land towards the center of the island. It was probably laughing at me for having to walk and not being able to fly. I was stunned by the realization that this was the first living creature besides the fish in the cove I had encountered so far on the island. I shuddered. I truly was alone on a deserted island.

After walking along the beach for about an hour, I could see the subtle shapes of the islands that Blaine and I walked across in the hazy distance. That was the path that led me to this island; to MY Island.

My heart started to race as I got closer to what I thought was the spot where Blaine and I camped those three long, frightening, and painful days. Was I really ready to come face to face with this again? I took a deep breath and pressed on; if I didn't do it now I never would.

I walked for another ten minutes or so when I started to feel déjà vu. It looked so familiar, yet there was no sign of the shelter Blaine and I built. There was no sign of the latrine area; no fire pit or plastic water bottles littering the beach like I thought there would be. It was weird. The area felt so familiar, yet nothing was right. I was sure this was the correct spot, but it was like someone or something had come behind us and cleaned it up. It didn't make sense.

As I scanned the area, I remembered our euphoric jubilation as we watched the rescue helicopter land on the beach. The crew quickly got out to confirm that we were the lost pilots they were looking for. They asked our names and gave Blaine some water. They had to insert an IV needle into me to get me rehydrated. Then we were in the air. We didn't clean up the island and we didn't take anything with us. We just left. We flew directly to the hospital on Majuro Atoll where we were both carefully examined by a doctor. Amazingly, we were in pretty good shape and were discharged from the hospital about five hours later.

I refocused on the mystery at hand. I was sure this was the area we were stranded in, so I began to systematically search the beach and bushes for signs of our previous occupation. I found a small piece of wrapper from the emergency food in the plane's survival kit and a plastic water bottle partially buried in the ground. Using a stick as a shovel, I was able to establish that our latrine had existed and had been covered up. I decided that when I got back to Majuro Atoll, I needed to talk with my rescuers and thank them for coming back and cleaning up. They did an excellent job. Seeing the beach all cleaned up with no remnants of the campsite somehow started to ease the pain of my memories.

The events of the crash still left me feeling rather unsettled. When our engines flamed out we began to fall in a controlled descent. It took us over an hour to descend after the last engine flamed out – plenty of time to wonder whether or not we would survive the landing. It was one hell of a bumpy ride all the way down since we had just entered into a thunderstorm cell. We sent out numerous distress calls, but we received no response from Majuro Atoll or any aircraft in the area at all.

None of my pilot's training prepared me for the sick feeling I had in my stomach as our plane belly-flopped on the water. How can anyone really prepare for the moment when you're scrambling to pull yourself out of a plane before it sinks to the bottom of the ocean?

It was not only scary to ditch the plane in a thunderstorm and then walk the many, many miles to the larger island – this island – it was terrifying to question whether or not we would ever be rescued. Because of the storm, we spent three days wondering if anyone had heard our mayday, and if a rescue team could actually find us, even if they were dispatched.

It turned out an aircraft had received our emergency signal, but we were unable to receive their response. There are no words to describe the relief we felt when we first caught sight of our rescue team.

As I looked down at my water supply I was shocked to discover I only had about a third of one bottle left. It was time to go back. I took one last look at the area that was our base camp after our crash, then turned and started the long trek home.

The walk back in the sweltering heat with only a little water made it seem longer and more arduous than the journey away. I was relieved when I came around the Dog Leg and could see my cove. It wouldn't be too long before I would be sitting in my living room and my favourite chair. That thought brought a smile to my face.

By the time I finally made it back home, I was truly exhausted. I dropped my GPS and empty water bottles on the table and went straight for the cooler. I grabbed two bottles of water. I swiftly twisted the cap off the first one and downed the whole thing in three massive gulps. I hurriedly twisted off the cap of the second and finished it as well. I let out an audible, "Ah!" and felt my body tingle in appreciation. With my thirst sated, I now seemed slightly less tired than just moments before.

Next hike, I'm going to have to take a lot more water with me. A smile crept across my face as it dawned on me: I'd actually thought "next hike" and not what I would have said just two or three months ago. The old me would have said, "I will never, ever go on another stupid hike like that again!" I chuckled; the heat had definitely made my brain soft.

I crushed my empty water bottles in a show of masculine aggression. Smirking like someone who had just accomplished some miracle, or a feat of intense concentration, I took my demolished bottles to the garbage bag and dropped them in. I walked back to the cooler to pull out a beer. I noticed the dry ice was still holding up nicely. I picked up some peanuts and walked to the living room. My body was dead-dog tired. I flopped into my chair and it groaned under my weight.

I sat there for a few moments, too worn out to move. Between setting up the awning and the very long walk in the intense heat, this had been a big day for me. I twisted the top off my icy cold beer, raised it in a salute to the ocean, and said, "Cheers! Here's to another beautiful sunset."

I took a slow, deliberate drink of the most delicious golden brown ale I had ever tasted. The liquid delight cooled my throat as it went down. After a day like I'd had, the beer was pure bliss. I smacked my lips in contentment and sighed, "Ahhh!"

I was content sitting in my beautiful open air living room. I looked out to the vastness of ocean until I was assaulted by a huge rain drop. I looked down at the leg of my shorts. *Wow! That has to be the largest rain drop in the world!* Plop! Another huge drop. I looked up and with impeccable timing, Plop! A drop hit me right in the middle of my forehead.

It was like my thoughts controlled the weather. The instant I thought, *I should get up, before the sky opens up and really dumps down on me.* The rain really began to dump down on me! I was completely and utterly drenched before I managed to stagger the 40 feet from my chair to the safety of the awning.

The one saving grace of getting drenched in the tropical rain is that the rain is warm. I stripped off my now soaked clothes and walked back out into the rain. It was like having a giant, lukewarm shower. I realized my soap was back in my tent but didn't want to risk flooding it, so I stood naked in the rain wondering what I could use as shampoo.

The rain eased off and became a gentle drizzle. By that time I smelled lemony fresh and was standing under the awning waiting for the rain to stop. I don't know if the makers of lemon scented dish soap thought people would use it as an emergency shower gel, but I thought it worked remarkably well. (Apart from the stinging when I got it in my eyes.)

I chuckled as I pictured a person standing in a public shower at some gym or public pool using a bottle of lemon dish soap as shower gel. I could picture the looks when people figured out what he was using. I doubled over in laughter as I imagined their dumbfounded stares. In my best Irish accent I said, "I use Lemony Fresh Dish Soap, don't you?" I howled in laughter at my own silliness.

When the rain stopped, I walked over to my tent to see if it had leaked. I unzipped it and peered inside. Dry as a bone! The money I spent on this quality tent was well worth it. Delighted, I stepped inside to put on some fresh clothes; I was starting to get cold. I also put my GPS away before returning to the kitchen. It was time for supper.

I decided to try out my new cast iron cooking pot to make a beef stew over the fire. First things first - I needed to build a fire. I was really glad I had chopped and covered a bunch of wood the day before. Thankfully, it was still dry. I wasn't really a fire-lighting kind of guy, so I needed this to be as easy as possible. Blaine had taken me out to the bush a couple times to practice my fire-lighting skills prior to coming to the island, but that was all the experience I had.

I had my kindling and wood piled just right. Or at least I hoped so. As insurance for my fledgling fire-lighting skills, I went over to my supply containers and got some Bar-B-Q lighter fluid which I poured generously over the firewood. I lit the match and threw it on the wood. Whoosh! I had the start of a perfect looking fire.

I stood back to admire my handy work as the fire tentatively took hold and slowly spread to light the larger logs. I glanced around and spied my beer back on the kitchen table. I grabbed it and turned in a salute toward the ocean. "Thank you, Blaine, for lecturing me about the importance of keeping my wood dry and for showing me how to build a fire." I smiled and raised my beer a second time. "Thank you, Sara, for suggesting I buy the lighter fluid." I took a slow, well-deserved drink.

I was feeling pretty good about myself as I returned to the kitchen. Today had been an exhausting day, but a really great one. I smirked, "I can tell Blaine the Boy Scout that I lit the fire with one match." As long as he didn't make me take a lie detector test on the one match story, I wouldn't have to admit to the Bar-B-Q fluid assistance and rat out Sara.

I set my beer down on the table and walked over to the coolers. It was time to make supper. I rummaged around for a few moments and gathered all the necessary ingredients for my beef stew. I was sure it was going to be the new island favourite.

I chuckled at my own joke then thought, *Oh, Graham; it's only been two days! What are you going to be like after 30 days by yourself?*

I dropped my armload of ingredients on the kitchen table with a resounding crash. In the relative silence of my rather tranquil setting this sudden noise seemed quite harsh. The waves rolling in on the beach about 50 feet away were the loudest noises I'd heard in the past two days, aside from the one sea gull I met today. I wondered how hard it would be to go back to the 'real' world in 28 days. My stomach gurgled and brought me out of my thoughts. I reached for a knife.

I had the beef, potatoes, carrots, and onions peeled and diced in short order. I put them in the pot and realized, much to my taste buds' horror that I hadn't brought out the spices. Back to the food containers. A good stew needed lots of pepper. A dash of this and a dash of that and presto! I had one great looking, mouthwatering stew. I sauntered over to the glowing fire, gently moved some logs around, and placed my new cast iron pot on the edge of the fire. I decided the fire needed a couple smaller logs so I walked over to the wood pile.

I froze and for just an instant, felt my heart in my throat. All around the wood pile were small shoe or boot prints. They were too small to be mine. Besides, I'd been bare foot

34

since the rain started. And they were fresh. I scanned the wood pile and tried to make sense of the shoe prints. Where did they come from? Nervously, I yelled, "Very funny, Blaine! You can come out now!" He could be playing a trick on me – at least I hoped it was Blaine. I was getting nervous. I turned and scanned the kitchen area. There were shoe prints over there too. I started to freak out! I watched enough reruns of C.S.I. to know that some of those shoe prints were made after I went to my supplies to get the spices. I tried to control the panic and quiver in my voice. "This isn't funny, Blaine or Sara! You can come out now!"

I frantically scanned the area for Blaine, Sara, Captain Taka, or his crew. As I turned away from the jungle I nearly jumped out of my skin. "Ack!!" Standing next to my chair, partially silhouetted in the setting sun, was a diminutive, scraggly, gray-haired man dressed in what looked to be a ragged Japanese World War II uniform! The sun setting behind him made it look like he had a golden glow surrounding him. Actually, it looked like the glow came from within him. It was weird and exceptionally unnerving.

I was chalking all this craziness up to the heat of the day and the beer. I blurted out, "Who are you? How did you get here? Why are you here?"

I didn't know if this little man was dangerous, but I was not taking any chances. I stood up a little taller and tried to make myself look menacing to make this tiny man think twice about robbing me, if that was his motive.

He simply offered me a smile that radiated warmth, trust, and compassion. Then he bowed very deeply and gracefully. It looked flawless. He stayed deep in his bow for a long time. When he slowly raised himself up from the waist again, he smiled and placed a hand on his heart. In slow and haltingly broken English he spoke. "Name, Akio."

Working on the Hawaiian Islands for as long as I had, I'd heard Japanese people speak English enough to know that my little island invader truly was of Japanese descent.

Akio stood there perfectly still, waiting patiently and expectantly of me. His gigantic, warm smile never left his face as waited. I stood there examining him.

He looked ancient. His hair hadn't seen a barber for years and his face was very weathered. His uniform had holes in both knees and there were buttons missing on his threadbare shirt. His brown boots were tattered and had large holes in the toes. His pants were held up by what looked like some sort of vine. It shocked me when I finally noticed that Akio was also wearing a sword.

Yet, for some reason, I no longer felt scared of him. I was actually feeling peaceful. It didn't make sense. A guy dressed in a tattered uniform with a sword had just walked into my camp on what was supposed to be a deserted island.

As Akio stood there on the beach, smiling that amazing smile, I continued to observe him. Despite his tattered and worn appearance, he stood before me with all the royalty, dignity, and grace of any king I had ever seen on TV.

It dawned on me that Akio was politely waiting for me to do something. As best as my portly body would allow, I stiffly bent at the waist and bowed. I almost fell over. I paused for a brief, painful moment, bent awkwardly at the waist, and then jerkily raised myself back up. I looked into Akio's eyes and said, "My name is Graham."

The next few moments will stay with me forever. The memory and sensations are permanently etched in my heart.

I slowly moved towards Akio, extending my right hand. He looked slightly perplexed as I stood before him with my hand extended. He hesitated and then ever so slowly took my hand. As our hands touched, the weirdest thing happened. I felt like I'd been touched by absolute love and acceptance. It sounds crazy, but the moment Akio touched my hand I felt as though I'd touched his heart and the heart of everyone else on the planet. It was overwhelmingly confusing and yet totally blissful; all at the same time.

We stood with our hands clasped for what seemed like an eternity before Akio softly asked, "No war?"

His question caught me completely off guard. I didn't know what war he was talking about. *No war? What war? The Gulf War? The War on Terrorism?* I asked, "What war?"

Akio took a deep breath. I looked into his eyes; they were filled with immense pain and hurt. Tears welled up, and I could almost feel his heart breaking. It was totally unsettling. I had never been able to feel anyone else's pain before.

Akio whispered, "War between Japan and United States for these islands."

It took just a second for the enormity of what he was asking to sink in. This dignified, old man in the tattered Japanese uniform was wondering if he was talking to his enemy.

Oh, man. The war ended in what? Think, Graham, think! Like 1946? I vaguely remembered studying the wars in school. The Marshall Islands were occupied by the Japanese in WWII and the U.S. liberated the islands around 1944. If I remembered right, it was really ugly and a lot of Japanese soldiers died.

Who thought any of the crap I learned in school would actually be useful? Shit! Why didn't I pay closer attention?

My head was swimming. Akio didn't know that the war had ended more than 60 years ago! He didn't know that his country lost. He had no idea how much the world had changed since then. Akio was a lost soldier of a bygone era, and now he was wondering if he was surrendering to me or if I was his prisoner. The incredibleness of the situation was mind-boggling.

Little by little, I regained my composure and thought processes. I looked Akio warmly in the eye. In my exuberant youth I know I would have said many unkind things to him. But there on the beach, I chose my words carefully. "Akio, the war is over. The United States and Japan are friends."

With surprising speed and dexterity, I caught Akio in my arms as he collapsed, sobbing under the enormity of my words. I gently lowered us to the sand. I can't say I could even begin to understand the depth of emotion Akio was going through, but I knew with complete certainty that my job was just to hold him and be with him. How I knew this, I couldn't guess, but I knew it just the same.

I also knew that this was the first time I'd ever truly cared about another human being. It had taken me 42 years to discover compassion. I found myself crying along with Akio, sharing in his grief and relief, as well as feeling the pain and sadness of my own life. I was started to understand how shallow my life really was.

I don't know how long I held Akio sobbing in my arms, but it was long enough for me to become very stiff and sore from sitting in the sand and for my roaring fire to burn down to a few small coals. Slowly and ever so gradually, I could feel the raw emotions losing their intense grip on Akio. His sobbing slowed. I could feel the wetness from his abundant tears soak through my shirt.

I felt Akio stir. Little by little, with an amazingly fluid grace, he stood up. He dusted off his tattered clothes, straightened his shirt and pants, and stood at attention. He crisply bowed to me and then offered me a heartfelt, "Thank you. Universe tell Akio war over long time. But Akio not believe. Akio now believe." I felt such warmth in his words, like a wave of kindness smothering my whole body.

Awkwardly and rather clumsily, I stood up and faced Akio. I bowed and simply said, "You're welcome." He seemed to internalize then accept my words. He responded with a huge impish grin.

Akio unhurriedly turned, walked over to the wood pile, picked up a few logs, and placed them gently on the fire. There was an enormous and really awkward silence between us. It reminded me of the "pillow scene" between John Candy and Steve Martin, in the movie *Planes, Trains and Automobiles.*

I didn't know what to say and I really didn't know what Akio would understand. Not knowing what else to do, I went back to preparing supper.

I walked over to my kitchen, pulled out the oven mitts and a large spoon to stir what I expected to be a burned and blackened beef stew. But when I lifted the lid and peered in, the aroma that poured out was heavenly. Akio looked so hungry I actually thought I saw him drooling. As I peered inside at the stew, it looked great. Amazingly, nothing looked burned! I carried the pot to the kitchen and took the lid off to allow the stew to cool for a few minutes. I walked over to my pile of storage containers, grabbed a couple of bowls, two spoons, and some bread. I rummaged in the coolers to grab each of us a bottle of water and a beer. Tonight we celebrate!

Before I dished out the stew, I went over to the wood pile and grabbed a few large logs. I stacked them just so, making a perfect bench next to my chair. I chuckled. I noticed Akio hadn't taken his eyes off the pot.

I dished out two big bowls of stew then placed a couple slices of bread on the side. I turned to Akio, waved him over, and picked up a hot bowl of stew. I offered it to him, "Would you like some stew?"

The look on Akio's face was priceless! It was absolute ecstasy.

He lovingly took the stew from me with both hands. He held the bowl out in front of his face, closed his eyes, smiled and then began to slowly breathe in the aroma. I think Akio stood there for almost five minutes just smelling the stew. Maybe not five minutes, but long enough for me to take Akio's water, beer, and spoon to the chair, set them on it, go get my own my dinner and drinks and take them to the makeshift bench and then get comfortably settled on it.

Akio was communing with his food. When he finally did open his eyes, he simply glanced around, discovered where I had gone, and walked over to the empty chair. He carried his bowl of stew like it was the most sacred of holy relics.

I grabbed the bottles of beer and water off the chair so Akio could sit down. He picked up the spoon from the chair and gently sat down. I twisted off the top of a bottle of water and handed it to him. Akio set his bowl and spoon in his lap and gracefully reached over to take the bottle from me. When his hand touched the cold bottle, he let out a squeal of childish delight. I glanced into Akio's face and it was awash with pure joy. He grinned at me and excitedly said, "Aaah! Tsume Tai!" He touched the cold, dripping bottle to his forehead and it dripped water onto his lap. "Tsume Tai!" he said again.

He turned to me with a mischievous grin and promptly splashed a little of his cold water on me. I screamed, "UUGHHH!"

Smiling gleefully, he raised the bottle of water over his head, titled his head back and poured water in his mouth and over his face, intermittently drinking and gargling what made it into his mouth. This was probably the coldest thing he had experienced in many, many years. I couldn't help but smile with Akio and feel his total glee over something as simple as cold water!

After playing with and drinking most of the bottle of water, Akio set it down in the sand making sure it wouldn't spill. Still smiling like the Cheshire Cat in *Alice in Wonderland*, he turned and faced the ocean. As I watched him, peacefulness seemed to envelope him and the whole area, ultimately melting into serene stillness.

Akio quietly picked up his bowl and spoon. He paused momentarily before he scooped out a spoon full of stew. He slowly and deliberately brought the hearty meal to his lips. He slurped it off the spoon and then his eyes flew open wide. "Karai!" He grabbed his water bottle and downed two huge gulps, emptying it. He sat feverishly smacking his lips, while frantically waving his hand in front of his open mouth, trying to cool the raging fire within. I could safely say that Akio was having difficulties with the pepper. I could see his eyes begin to water. I handed him my water bottle which he snatched from my hand and gulped from.

I said, "Akio, eat the bread," and motioned to show him what I meant.

Suspiciously, Akio took a small bite of bread. He smiled as he tasted it; he then took a larger bite. Bread helped me to take away the spicy inferno of pepper, and I hoped it would do the trick for Akio. I could see beads of sweat forming on his forehead. He turned to me and with a look that I can only describe as mock seriousness said, "You say war over! Why you try kill me?"

We both roared out loud. I almost dropped my stew as I doubled over in fits of laughter.

Despite the spiciness, Akio managed to eat his bowl of stew and at least half a loaf of bread to counter the effects of the pepper. I enjoyed watching him savour his meal as much as I enjoyed eating my own.

Content from filling our bellies, we just sat and stared out at the vast emptiness of the crystal blue ocean in silence.

I reached down and grabbed one of the beer bottles. When I twisted off the cap, the familiar *phssssatt* of the seal breaking interrupted Akio's rapture with the ocean. He turned to see what I was doing. I handed him the bottle, and he took it from me somewhat reluctantly. After opening mine, I turned and faced the ocean. I raised my beer in a salute and said, "Cheers!" Then shifting to face Akio, I reached over and tapped the two bottle necks together before raising mine once again in a salute. This time my salute was to Akio. For the second time, I said, "Cheers!" and then lifted the bottle to my lips. I took a sip of the golden nectar and sighed contentedly.

Akio looked somewhat perplexed, but he began to duplicate my actions. After offering all of the "Cheers", he raised his bottle to his lips and took a tiny, tentative sip. He let out a roar in celebration. "Aaaaahhhhh!" Akio turned to me with a huge grin plastered on his face. He obviously enjoyed his first taste of beer in a very long time, perhaps ever. He raised his beer once again in salute and offered, "Cheers!" taking another long, slow drink.

Day Three

I was struggling to come to some sense of recognition. *Where am I? What is going on?* I could hear a foreign voice off in the distance, "Up, Graham! Up, Graham!"

My brain was filled with a thick, gooey, gelatinous mist. My head was swimming with foggy images of an old Japanese soldier, sunset, stew, and beer. Lots and lots of beer. Me and this Japanese man dancing around the fire, howling, singing…and more beer. I stirred, moving my arms slightly. My stomach churned.

I tried looking around, but I couldn't focus. It was like I had a sticky film glued to my eyes. I could almost see the old man from my dreams in front of me, yelling, "Up, Graham!" My mouth was dry – it felt like the sand my camp was sitting on. My tongue felt the size of a giant grapefruit. The back of my throat felt raw and raspy. I tried to move my fog-filled head, struggling to get a better look at the man that appeared to be talking to me.

As I struggled to raise my body to an upright position, the world began to swirl. *Yup! Graham Connelly, you are SO hung over.*

Slowly, and very cautiously, I moved to an upright position. I sat still for what seemed like a long time. If I didn't look down or move quickly, things seemed not too bad. That wasn't exactly a problem; I was hardly even capable of moving, let alone moving quickly.

Gingerly, I looked around to find the voice that kept moving around and yelling, "Up, Graham, Up!" I peered through my bleary, bloodshot eyes and saw an old Japanese soldier moving towards me. I thought I saw a long, shiny stick in his hand. *No, it looked more like a sword. Now why would someone have a sword in their hand on a beach? My beach! Very strange. Very strange indeed.*

I was sitting upright with a ridiculously foolish grin on my face, ever so sluggishly trying to process a man with a sword on my beach when suddenly I felt a searing pain shoot though my leg and I heard a resounding *thwack.*

The sword connected with my leg, and the pain cleared the foggy mist from my head. "What are you doing, Akio?" I screeched.

Akio simply yelled back, "Up, Graham!" Then he raised his sword to strike me again. Groggily, I tried to stand, my head spinning and my stomach churning. I couldn't focus. My legs were shaky. I heard Akio yell once more, this time in a very large, commanding voice, "Up, Graham, Up!" I struggled to turn and face him, but he kept moving around and I was having difficulty following him.

Out of the corner of my eye, I saw the flat of Akio's sword come whizzing towards me again. The flat of the blade struck the side of my leg. Pain exploded through my body.

Angrily, I shot my body straight up, wildly grabbing at the weapon. I wanted to get the thing and beat him with his own damn sword!

Akio gracefully side-stepped my wild grab for the sword and with the same grace and skill, promptly hit me again on the same thigh. "Good!" he yelled boisterously, taking a step backwards and raising the sword again. I lunged forward. I was going to get that damn thing out of his hands if it killed me! I was furious. I'd fed him, I drank beer with him, we sang songs, and now this little old man was beating me with a sword on my island.

Wobbly, I advanced. Akio fluidly stepped backwards. When I lunged forward he took three graceful steps back. I could feel my balance returning. I charged forward like I was crazed. My legs were bursting with aggression. I closed in on Akio. I was determined to get that sword.

I was no longer Graham Alexander Connelly, I was Graham the Cheetah. I was the fastest hunter on the island. As I sprang forward, frantically grasping for the sword, Akio - in what appeared to be one fluid motion - simply side stepped my charge, extending his right leg and hip. He sent me sprawling to the ground. Adding further insult to injury, Akio swatted my ass with the sword as I flew by him.

I hastily picked myself up. I turned to face Akio and through clenched teeth I demanded, "Give me that damn sword!"

Akio looked at his sword, turned to me, then looked back at his sword. He smiled and held it out. "Want sword? Take!" was all he said. I reached for the sword and as I did, Akio pulled it back, spun it around, placed it in its scabbard, and jogged away from me.

When I recovered from the shock, I started running after him. I wanted that damn sword!

I had run about twenty feet when I began laughing to myself. I had him now! I could taste victory. Akio was at least twice my age. I knew I could outrun an 80-something year old man. I poured on the speed. Once again I was Graham the Cheetah. I quickly closed the gap between us. I was about five feet behind him. I could feel that sword in my hands. I inched my way closer and closer. Four feet behind Akio... three feet behind. I could almost grab him by his shoulders.

Akio glanced over his shoulder, smiled when he saw how close I was and simply said, "Good! Come!"

He effortlessly picked up his pace. I think I came close to tripping over my jaw as it dropped in utter amazement. I was a hung-over, 42 year old running flat out trying to chase a skinny, little ancient man and I couldn't do it. I was absolutely astounded. I couldn't even outrun a little old man.

Akio was pulling away from me like I was standing still. I felt the testosterone kick in. Pride was coursing through my veins. I pushed myself harder and gave it everything I had.

Once again, I was closing the gap. Ten feet, nine feet, eight feet… I was getting closer.

Akio abruptly stopped, spinning around to face me. He had a huge, playful grin on his face. I uncontrollably stumbled to a stop, barely managing to stay upright. Akio deftly withdrew the sword from its scabbard, and raised it shoulder height. He held it out to me horizontally, holding the middle of the blade with both hands.

But before I could take the sword, I had to catch my breath. I stood panting and wheezing, just three feet in front of my goal. But I was physically unable to take the sword. As I was doubled over gasping for air, I glanced back towards camp to see how far we had run. It was only about 200 yards! I was pathetically out of breath and out of shape.

Akio just stood there holding the sword out, waiting patiently for me to catch my breath and take it from him. He looked at me and asked, "How you head? Clear?"

It took a few seconds for his question to register, but yes, my head was clear. Getting slapped with a sword multiple times and then running down a beach like a mad man seemed to have cured my hang over. It wasn't a remedy that I would highly recommend, but it did work.

I stood straight. I looked Akio in the eyes and reached to take the sword from him. He simply said, "Careful, sharp!" I admired the detail of the sword for a few minutes, appreciating its feel, weight and balance. I had never actually held a sword before.

Akio broke my admiration of the sword by saying, "Graham, get two sticks same size as sword, please!" He pointed towards the jungle and slowly (and rather deliberately, I suspected) turned his back on me to face the ocean.

As I stood there staring at Akio with my mouth open, I realized I was no longer angry at him. The pain and the sudden burst of exercise had loosened the grip the alcohol held on my body. I didn't know why he beat me, but as I stood holding the sword in my hands, I was no longer tempted by revenge. The notion of beating Akio had passed. I shook my head in utter bewilderment and set off to get the sticks.

I returned to the beach less than ten minutes later, hot and sweaty from the exertion. It had been quite a struggle to find the right diameter of branches in the tropical jungle. I saw Akio standing in the same spot where I had left him, looking out over the ocean. I went and stood beside him. He turned slightly as I approached and I could see a smile on his face. It was replaced with a serious look of concern. "How head?" he asked.

All I could say was, "Good."

Akio then raised his hands to represent claws and contorted his face to that of some possessed wild animal. With a snarl he said, "Graham? Grarrarr!" His faced shifted into his impish little smile, "Or Graham?" He exaggerated a huge smile which somehow encompassed his whole body.

It took me a second or two to realize that he was asking me whether I was still angry with him or if I was happy. All I could do was smile. I still didn't like that he hit me to get me up, but now that I was up and standing here with him, things were okay.

Akio turned and faced me. "Sword," he demanded, and held out his hands. I lifted the sword to hand it back to him and he yelled, "No!"

I was so startled I nearly dropped the sword. I didn't understand his abrupt and apparently random behaviour. But when I looked searchingly into his eyes I could tell he was trying to figure something out. He was trying to decide what to say or do next.

It felt very weird watching him. He could shift instantly from an abrupt, crisp, commanding person to a soft and caring one. He was as gentle as some people become around babies, as if his insides had gone mushy.

Akio removed the scabbard from his belt and carefully handed it to me. "Graham, put sword," he said. I slid the sword into the scabbard and tried to hand it back. He smiled and shook his head. Again, he simply said, "No." He motioned for me to place the sword on the ground beside us.

Akio pointed to the two sticks I had selected from the jungle and said "Graham, take one." I picked one up. He frowned, then with a chiding tone said, "Graham, watch." With an almost perfect swagger, Akio mimicked the way I stood and walked. He staggered over and rather clumsily picked up the stick. I couldn't help but laugh at the comical way he did it.

Then I stopped laughing. If I had done what Akio just showed me, it was obvious I wasn't very graceful. If I saw someone move like that, I'd probably laugh at them.

Akio smiled, dropped the stick back into the sand, and walked back to his original spot. As he faced me he said, "Graham, watch!" He very smoothly and purposefully walked to the stick. He moved as though he could walk through water without causing even the slightest ripple. He stopped in front of the stick, but instead of picking it up, he turned to face me and asked, "Graham, you have woman?"

I muttered, "No."

Akio then looked deeply into my eyes. It felt like he was boring a hole inside my head. He crisply asked, "Graham, you…?" He seemed lost for words, but made hitting motions.

In shock, I emphatically replied, "No!" I wondered where this question came from.

"Graham, you treat woman nice?"

"Yes!"

Akio seemed pleased with my answer. A huge smile exploded across his face. I couldn't help myself, I had to smile too. I didn't know why, but I was smiling none the less.

Akio just stood silently for a moment; he appeared to be collecting his thoughts. Then with the look of a person who had just won the lottery, he said, "Graham, you nice to women?"

I responded with a slow and puzzled, "Yes," wondering where his thought process was going.

"Graham nice to women, but not nice to all!" Akio bent down and scooped up some sand and repeated himself, "Graham nice to women, but not nice to all." He began to pour the sand over my hand and excitedly said, "But all is woman!"

He opened his palm to show me the remaining sand in his hand and exclaimed, "This woman." Then he pointed to the stick, "Woman!" Then he ran into the ocean, excitedly splashing, "This Woman!" Next he pointed to some nearby rocks, "This woman!" Running like an excited child who was just let out of school for the summer, he ran to the edge of the jungle and pointed to the trees, the bushes, the insects, all the while squealing, "This woman!" Akio's exuberance was so infectious I had to catch myself; I was almost going to break out in song, singing *Woman* by David Gates and *Bread*.

I think I was starting to get Akio's point. He was saying that all around me, nature was "woman." He must have sensed that I understood because he quit running around.

Akio, still smiling, walked over and gracefully picked up one of the sticks I had selected for him. He proceeded to draw something in the sand. I peered over his shoulder at his drawing, and it appeared to be a picture of our galaxy. There was the sun, the planets, and Earth. Akio excitedly looked up to me and pointed his stick to the third planet in our galaxy and said, "Woman."

It was when Akio pointed his stick to the planet earth that I got some sense of the enormity of what he was trying to tell me. For the first time in my life I understood, at some basic fundamental level, the true meaning of the phrases 'Mother Nature' and 'Mother Earth'. It was like a giant light bulb went off in my head. Akio was trying to tell me that our earth, 'Mother Nature' or 'Woman' as he referred to it, was special and I should treat it that way. I couldn't think of how to tell Akio that I understood. All I could think to do was yell at the top of my lungs, "Woman!" and point to everything around me. Akio was smiling with recognition. He knew I got the point.

I felt a need to show Akio that I really understood. I needed to pick up the stick with respect. No, not just respect. I needed to have a dignified walk, some sense of ceremony to the act, some form of honour toward that stick. I needed to pick it up like it was sacred.

Ding, Ding, Ding! It was like a whole bunch of bells went off inside my head. I suddenly realized I need to treat all things like they were sacred. That was what Akio was trying to teach me. I didn't treat anything other than food as if it was sacred. I truly took most things for granted.

I knew now with absolute certainty that I needed to treat that stick as a sacred object. With my heart beating about 900 miles an hour with excitement and absolute joy, I looked into Akio's eyes. I gently said, "Akio, watch."

Very purposefully, I walked towards the stick. In my mind it symbolized all things sacred to me - love, compassion, friendship, laughter, and even food. With the care and tenderness a father would pick up his newborn child, I bent down to pick up the stick. Just before I touched it, I stopped, straightened my back and stood up.

Holding on to the same feeling of sacredness, I walked over to where we left Akio's sword and reverently picked it up. I held on to the sword as if all of mankind's essence rested within that very blade. Slowly, I turned and faced Akio. I purposefully strode over to him and stopped just in front of him. I grasped the middle of the scabbard and held the sword out horizontally. Respectfully, I lifted the sword to my shoulder height and waited for Akio to take it from me.

Akio stood calmly and peacefully before me. He looked deeply into my eyes and smiled a huge smile of recognition. He knew I understood what he was trying to teach me. His smile made me feel like I was loved. I don't know how else to describe it. And as wonderful as it was, it also felt really weird for me, because men don't love men, at least not in my family.

Akio reached up to take the sword and scabbard from me. He carefully and deliberately reattached it to his makeshift belt. Once the sword and scabbard were back where they belonged, he bent at the waist and gave me a deep and gracious bow. He rose and looked me in the eye. I could sense he was formulating words. Akio struggled to piece together his sentence, "Graham, how you now act?"

I heard the question, and even though my brain registered it, I had no idea how to answer him. Out of habit, I wanted to give some off-the-cuff, totally glib answer. But some newly blossoming part of my being wanted to answer Akio's question from a softer, kinder, more heart-felt place.

I looked at Akio and smiled. "Akio, the answer for me is to treat life with reverence and treat things more sacredly."

Akio frowned. I knew it was from lack of understanding and not disappointment. I tried again. "Akio, I will treat things as if they come from, or are part of, a temple."

The instant I spoke the word 'temple' Akio's face lit up. He even broke out into a little dance. And in the midst of his unabashed 'happy dance,' Akio said, "Good word, TEMPLE!"

Akio danced his happy dance for a few more seconds, then stopped and smiled at me. "Graham no smile enough. Need more smile!" Akio pointed to the stick on the ground and said, "Get stick with smile in body."

For some crazy reason, I felt compelled to do my best limbo dance steps to retrieve my stick. Akio absolutely loved it! He was laughing while doing his best to imitate my steps. I must admit, the 'new me' thought it was a lot of fun. The old Graham, on the other hand, would have been absolutely horrified with my current behaviour. It was very important for the old Graham to always appear in complete control. It was a sign of weakness not to be in control at all times.

After a few more moments of our silly dancing, Akio said, "Good smile, Graham. Come stand here." He pointed to a spot about three feet directly in front of him. I moved over to the spot Akio indicated and as I stood there, I realized I still had a smile plastered all over my face.

I stood in front of Akio and he became serious. It was interesting to note the subtle and minute changes - the changes in the smile lines on his face and the ever so slight change in his posture. I was amazed by the process. I had never before been present enough to notice the little changes one goes through as thought and feelings shift. I had to smile. I now realized why Sara was so wise; she really saw people.

I realized that Akio was watching me. He recognized I was lost in thought and was patiently waiting for me to come back to the moment. I refocused on Akio so that he could continue on with whatever he wanted to teach me.

With a serious expression, Akio pointed towards his body, "Temple." Then he pointed towards my body, "Temple."

I could sense he was formulating a new concept; he had a troubled look on his face. Akio looked at me and said, "Graham big temple. Graham need be small temple. Graham need fix temple."

In a blinding flash of anger the old Graham flooded back; resentment poured into me. *Who the hell does this old man think he is? What right does he think he has to come here and drink my beer, beat the crap out of me, and now tell me I'm too fat? That's pure bull crap!* I was enraged. I felt my muscles tighten and my breathing quicken. I was ready to beat someone! My desire to beat Akio returned with a vengeance. I picked up my stick, poised, ready to strike. I wanted him to feel my raw anger, my desire to hurt him and hurt him badly. I wanted to cripple the old man.

I raised my stick to strike. Akio raised his to counter. Yet, as I stared deep into his eyes, I didn't sense any fear. Akio wasn't afraid of what I may do to him nor of how this situation would turn out. Instead, I sensed his incredible strength.

My delay in starting the fight gave the new Graham a chance to find his voice. *Graham, everything is sacred. Akio has not said anything to you that is not true. Your body temple IS too big.*

The battle raged within me. I still had my sword raised and ready to strike. Akio hadn't moved. He was poised and ready to counter.

58

I stared deeply into Akio's eyes. Again, I became aware of the subtle changes in his body. The smile lines on his face softened. He relaxed his stomach muscles and started to slouch ever so slightly. I sensed he was trying to show me something.

My body began to tingle. It was like a little breeze gently caressed my face. Ever so slowly, it crept into my body and my consciousness. The tsunami suddenly washed over me – a wave of pure, raw emotion. I realized that no matter how much pain I could or would inflict on Akio, he would still love me no matter what.

I dropped my sword and crumpled to the sand. I had never truly felt love before, let alone unconditional love. I was never really loved as a child. I never felt that no matter how poorly I behaved, someone could and would love me. I can't remember ever being told "Job well done!" or "I'm proud of you son!" I don't think my father ever hugged me, not even once! The only thing my father gave me was the back of his hand or a whipping with his belt.

I was openly weeping. I felt Akio come sit next to me. I looked into his face and saw it awash with pure love. Tears were streaming down his cheeks as well.

Akio sat beside me and allowed me to weep. I cried for how my parents treated me as a child. I cried for how I treated them as I grew older. I cried for how I treated people who tried to be my friends. I cried for my relatives who tried to help, but I pushed them away in fear. I cried harder when I thought of how poorly I treated Blaine and Sara. My sorrow turned to tears of joy as I realized how much I really loved them. Yes! I used the "L" word. *Yes! I do love Blaine and NO! I am not gay. And yes, I do love Sara.*

Once it was allowed in, that revelation expanded. Sara filled my thoughts. I had more than a passing interest in her. I was surprised that I longed for more than just a romance. I wanted a long term relationship. For a second, the old Graham found his voice. Eeewwwww!

When my tears eventually ran out, Akio and I just sat on the beach staring out at the ocean. Each wave that washed onto the shore seemed to pull my pain and sorrow out to the sea and bring a new sense of awareness to me. The only sound I was aware of was the rhythm of the surf. For the first time since I arrived on the island I could taste the salt in the air. I could smell the pungent sea weed odor and the sweet smell of the land. Palm trees have a sweet smell. *Who knew?*

It was my stomach that finally broke our silence with a gurgle and growl. I turned to Akio with a smile, "Food?"

"Soon," Akio nodded. "Graham, Akio have no answer why hit you to wake up. It feel like right thing to do. Akio alone much time on island; learn to listen to Universe. Learn to know, not think. Akio not think about hit you; know hit Graham to wake up. I do what I know. Graham, forgive Akio?"

I smiled and nodded my head, "Yes."

He returned my smile and nodded. We both quietly stood up. I loosened my belt and slid the stick which nearly served as a sword between my belt and pants. We walked back to camp in silence.

When we got back to camp, the first thing I did was show Akio where the bottled water and food supplies were stored. I rummaged around and got out all the ingredients for my favourite island breakfast – fried potato hash and coffee. I began to prepare the food and was struck with a brain wave. When I was buying my supplies the store clerk threw in a package of loose green tea. "To help digestion," she said. I bet Akio was more of a tea than coffee kind of guy. So I got out a pot to boil water. In no time flat, I had the coffee made and water boiling for tea.

Akio had the living room cleaned up and all the bottles picked up in short order. He even put them away in the bags I brought for the recyclables. I remembered the argument Sara and I had about bringing back the bottles. I was just going to bury them, but she was adamant that I bring them back. So much so that she wasn't going to let me go on this adventure until I promised I would leave nothing behind. Sara actually threatened to cancel my holiday request over a few plastic bottles! Thinking of Sara brought a little smile to my face.

Akio took the axe and wandered into the jungle. I could hear him chopping behind me. He returned to camp every few minutes, dragging a small tree or branch. Before breakfast was ready, Akio had several trees stacked neatly by the wood pile.

I finished brewing Akio a cup of green tea. I scooped a couple hearty mounds of fried potatoes and eggs onto each of our plates. It looked sumptuous. I couldn't wait to devour every last bite. With care, I took Akio's food and a mug of tea to the living room and placed them on the folding chair. I went back for my own plate and a cup of coffee then sat on the logs next to his chair. I heard Akio come up behind me. He came around and faced me. He was carrying the pan I cooked our breakfast in. He placed it on his chair, smiled at me, and then gently took my plate. I was puzzled.

With my plate in one hand he reached down, took the fork I was holding, and then efficiently scraped a portion of my meal back into the pan. It looked like he left me with about 80% of the meal. With a look of sincere understanding and compassion Akio said, "Small temple, small food," and handed my plate back.

Akio picked up his plate and quickly scraped at least half of his meal back into the pan. He turned to me and said, "Akio eat much last night. Akio sick this morning. Now eat small food."

I was a bit shocked when I saw my food scraped back into the pan, but I was relieved that he didn't just dump it on the ground or into the fire. At least it wouldn't go to waste; we could save it for tomorrow.

I might have been really annoyed with having my meal portion controlled for me if I was not anxiously waiting to see Akio's reaction over the tea. I expected this to be his first in many, many years.

I didn't have long to wait before Akio raised his cup to his lips, slowly and deliberately inhaling the aroma from his cup. His reaction was instant, like a dam bursting. This time I not only saw the physical changes to Akio's body, but I felt the internal changes in him as well. I saw his bottom lip begin to quiver. I saw the skin around his eyes tighten and the tears begin to roll down his face. Akio slowly turned his head to me and quietly spoke, "Graham, tea big in Japan. Big honour with tea. I leave for war, Mother pour tea. Last tea I drink. Tea make many memories."

Tears now coursed down Akio's face as I reached over and tentatively touched the tea cup. Little by little, Akio released his grip. I gingerly took the cup from him. Carefully holding it, I stood and walked a few paces towards the ocean. I paused there for a few moments, finding the feeling that everything is sacred and should be treated as such. Just as yesterday, the feeling of carrying a sacred relic rose in my body. I walked purposefully towards Akio, stopping directly in front of him. "Akio, I don't know any tea ceremonies, but would you like a cup of tea?" I reverently held out his cup, partially bowing to him in the process.

Akio looked at me with a huge smile; one that I will remember for a very, very long time. He simply bowed and said, "Yes." He gently took the cup from my hands and raised it to his lips to take a small sip.

We ate in silence, once again enjoying the calming sound of the ocean. When we finished our breakfast we both just sat in our respective chairs, absorbed in our own thoughts. Akio eventually broke the solitude, "Good Tea. Thank You."

I replied with a warm, "You are welcome," and we settled back into our comfortable silence.

My butt eventually got too sore to sit any longer, so I stood up and took our dishes to the kitchen. Akio followed me. I showed him how to light the stove and we began heating water for dishes and for more tea for Akio. He took two bottles of water from the cooler and we finished them as we waited for the dish water.

In no time at all, we had our dishes done and the kitchen was all cleaned up. Akio walked over to one of the ropes I had tied the awning up with and asked, "Graham, small rope?" He pointed to the rope.

Figuring he was looking for a smaller piece of rope, I said, "Yes," and waved for him to follow me. I showed Akio the container where the rope, string, saw, and machete were stored. He took some string, the saw, and the machete, then carefully closed the lid.

Akio walked over and picked up the stick I had cut for him. Using the saw, he cut off both ends to make them blunt rather than pointed. He picked up a coconut – Where did that come from? – and with the saw he made a small cut. Then raising the coconut to his lips, he began to noisily suck the sweet juice through the gash. Once it was empty, he skillfully sawed all the way through the coconut. What he created looked like a small, roundish saucer.

Akio walked over to the supply containers and systematically rummaged through the cutlery box until emerging victoriously with a large, sharp knife. He sported an "I found it!" grin. He returned to his coconut saucer. He placed the knife point into the middle of the saucer and began to use it like a drill to put a hole in the hard coconut shell.

I walked back to the cooler and got us a couple more bottles of water. I placed Akio's beside him so as not to interrupt his work. I sat down on the sand across from him. He had me intrigued; what he was making? It took a lot of effort on his part, but he soon had a hole through the middle of the coconut saucer that was about two inches in diameter.

Akio paused for a sip of water, and then retrieved the stick with the now blunt ends. He placed the small saucer over top of it and slid it down. "You're making a guard for the sword!" I said excitedly. Akio smiled and simply nodded. The hole in the guard needed to be bigger to fit in the proper position, so he removed it and continued to fine tune the diameter of the hole.

"Are you making an edge on the sword?" I asked him.

Akio shook his head, "No edge. Practice sword."

After about ten more minutes of delicate carving, Akio's guard was firmly in place on his new practice sword. He stood and began slowly swinging it in giant figure eights. He swung it first to the right and then to the left. I wasn't sure, but it looked like he was swinging it in a pattern. Akio seemed pleased with his results. He stopped his graceful movements, looked over at me and said, "Graham, you make now."

What looked like an easy process was not. I was just going to chop the end of my stick off and slide on the guard, but that wasn't good enough. Akio coaxed and coached me through an exacting process of weighting the stick properly. If the guard was in the wrong place it would change the balance of my sword. Everything had to be in balance.

Carving the hole in the coconut was a skill; one I appeared to be utterly incompetent at. What took Akio maybe twenty minutes to carve took me over two hours and three coconuts. I thought it was pretty good at about the 65 minute mark and coconut number two, but it was not good enough for Master Akio.

Master Akio? Where the hell did that come from?! Have I watched too many Kung Fu movies? I chuckled to myself. *Master Akio! As IF!*

I held up my sword, admiring my handy work. My fingers ached, but I had to admit that Akio was right. It was much better and looked a lot nicer than the mess I had created over an hour ago.

Master Akio walked over to the storage containers and returned with some rope and a couple bottles of water. Together we created a belt to hold the sword around my waist.

I thanked Master Akio for the water and took a couple swigs from the bottle. I must have sweated at least a quart of water building that sword.

I suddenly felt very tired. I took my bottle of water to my bench and sat down. *Graham, you've got to stop with the Master Akio stuff!*

What a crazy day! So much had happened already. I felt completely foreign in my very stiff and sore body, yet I was more alive than ever before. I felt like I was me and yet I wasn't me. "Graham, this heat is definitely making your head mushy," I said out loud.

"What Graham say?" Master Akio asked me. I was a little bit embarrassed about talking out loud so I hastily responded, "Sorry, Master Akio, I was talking to myself." I raised my bottle to my lips to take a sip of water, but paused part way. Did I just say the words 'Master Akio' out loud? I turned my head slightly towards him. I could tell by the profound look on his face that I had not only said it out loud, but he fully understood what I said.

Akio stopped chopping the tree he had been working on. He put the axe down and strolled over to sit beside me. Akio became very solemn, "Graham, master and student very, very serious. Master job teach, but not give answers. Student job, learn, no matter how Master teach. Student job very hard."

I looked at Akio and told him it was just an accident that I had called him 'Master'; I didn't really mean it.

He smiled, pausing for a long time before he spoke. "No, Graham. No accident Graham crash here. No accident Graham come back. No accident Akio follow Graham. No accident Graham say 'Master'." He paused. "What Graham heart say?"

That was an interesting question. I had never before had anyone ask me what my heart said. I pondered it, taking a couple of slow, deliberate sips of water while formulating my response. "The old Graham says no! The new Graham says yes to Master Akio."

This time when I spoke the words 'Master Akio' out loud it somehow felt right; yet weird at the same time. From somewhere deep inside I heard the deafening click of a giant padlock unlocking followed by a huge set of doors creaking open. It felt like a hidden passage in my life had been opened. Something strange was going on and I wasn't sure about any of it.

Akio smiled an impish, knowing smile. "We talk more tomorrow. Stand up, Graham. Bring sword."

I stood up and we both walked towards the ocean, stopping on the beach just past the living room. Akio had me face him. We stood approximately four feet apart.

"Graham, do what Akio do," Master Akio said.

He bowed, so I bowed. He drew his sword from his scabbard, moving his right foot back a small step. He held the sword with his right hand snug up to the guard, while his left hand held the very bottom of the grip. His hands were spaced so that they were not touching. I had seen enough movies to know that this was the legendary samurai pose. I mimicked his stance and hand positions.

Master Akio showed me how to strike straight over-the-head and then how to counter that overhead blow. Over and over, Master Akio commanded, "Strike, block, strike, block." We practiced just those two moves for over an hour before he called an end to our lesson.

"Graham good student. Now go in ocean, wash, then eat."

"Yes! I like that idea!" I joyfully exclaimed.

I carried my now christened sword back to our living room, carefully placing it on the bench. I quickly shed my extremely sweaty clothes and piled them neatly on the bench beside my sword. Then, like a kid on Christmas morning, I bolted for the warm ocean water, crashing head long into the waves. I don't think I will ever get tired of jumping into waves and getting washed ashore.

It wasn't long before Master Akio joined me and we were both body surfing to the shore, all the while laughing ourselves silly. Prior to coming to the island I had never laughed so much or for so long. It felt good to laugh.

I was suddenly struck with the desire to put my thoughts into my journal. *Might as well use it since Sara went to all the trouble to buy it for me.* As soon as lunch was over I would begin.

There were certain advantages to being overweight. The waves didn't sweep me off my feet as dramatically as they did Master Akio. He was, at most, 120 pounds, soaking wet. The waves effortlessly flipped him over and launched him high on to shore. He simply picked up his sinewy little body and ran back in for more.

After almost crashing into each other for about the tenth time, Master Akio looked over at me, his white hair disheveled, water dripping off his face. He smiled and said, "Eat now?" I nodded in agreement.

I walked to the tent for towels and some clothes for both of us. I returned and found Master Akio standing in the sun, allowing his body to dry. I handed him a towel and he gratefully took it from me. Once again, I was awestruck by his ability to revel in the simplest of pleasures - a soft towel.

Master Akio held the towel to his face for a long time and then slowly ran it over his entire body enjoying every single second of the experience. As I watched him, I became subtly aware of what it meant to be grateful. I had so many things, even here on the island that I took completely for granted. I hadn't ever thought about being grateful for what I had. This dear, old, skinny man was teaching me without saying a word. When Master Akio finished communing with his towel, he looked over to me. Contentment was pasted on his face. I pointed to the clothes I brought from the tent and said, "Try them on. They will be too big for you, but at least they won't be rags."

Master Akio picked up the shorts and once again began to smile like a kid in a candy store. He quickly put them on and figured out how to use the draw string. He slipped the t-shirt on and although it was at least two sizes too large for him, he seemed pleased. I had to laugh at the irony of the shirt he was wearing. I bought it on the beach in Hawaii, thinking I was being smart when I wore it around Blaine. It said, "I'm with Stupid."

I was very aware that my new temple (that is, my body) was going to get smaller portions for a while, so I chose to create our meal with smaller portions in mind. I knew Master Akio would just scrape the food off my plate if I took too much, so that made my decision to prepare smaller portions pretty easy.

I diced some chicken and boiled brown rice that took forever to cook because Master Akio kept lifting the lid to smell it. I threw it all together with some carrots and peas and presto! We had a great tasting stir-fry. Master Akio made tea and we even had half a can of fruit cocktail for dessert.

We took our food to the living room and sat in our respective chairs, silently looking out into Sara's Cove. My body was exhausted and tired, but my mind was fully alive and alert. It felt like my whole brain was tingling... tingling with possibility. I was learning to live life. For the first time, I was excited about life - *my* life, to be more precise.

I emerged from my new-found bliss to ask Master Akio, "Plans for this afternoon?"

"No," he replied without taking his eyes off the ocean.

We sat mesmerized by the hypnotic sounds of the waves crashing to the shore in front of us for a long time. Eventually, I broke from my revelry and stood to take my dishes to the kitchen. Master Akio spoke, "Graham cook, Akio clean."

"Okay," I said. I left the dishes near the wash basins and went to the tent to get my journal.

I entered the sauna, an appropriate nickname for my tent. It felt like it was about 120° F with 99% humidity inside. I spied my journal right away. I picked it up and realized I still had not found the pen Sara said accompanied it. If my memory served me right, I needed to look in the beer cooler.

I rummaged through the cooler for a long time before I found a small colourful package encased in plastic. The present was smothered in the dry ice near the bottom of the cooler. I smiled to myself as I closed the lid. Sara's thoughtfulness and resourcefulness amazed me. How she got a pen in my beer cooler was a mystery. I bought all my groceries in advance of arriving at Majuro Atoll. I remember asking Sara to check over my list before I faxed it to the supply store. The sneak must have added the pen to the list, or faxed in her own order. Either way, she was pretty organized to get a pen in my beer cooler from so far away.

I took my plastic-wrapped treasure to the kitchen to get the scissors so I could unwrap it. Master Akio, with his hands still wet from washing the dishes, saw that I was up to something and walked over to see what. I looked up at him as he was curiously eyeing the package. "A gift from a friend," I said.

Master Akio smiled. "Woman friend?"

I blushed slightly and responded, "Yes." He gave me a big grin and looked down at the package excitedly, willing me to open it faster. I slowly cut off the plastic, revealing a well wrapped package. Maybe it was my personal bias, but I didn't think it was as neatly wrapped as my journal. I was pretty sure that someone other than Sara had wrapped it. Carefully, I peeled the tape off both ends and slid out the small box. The simple white box was taped closed. I cut the tape with the scissors.

Once again, I found myself in a weird emotional place. This was the second time in a couple days I was opening a present and I was doing it with care. I was actually savoring the moment; taking pleasure in the unknown. Yes, I knew it was a pen inside, but I didn't know what kind of pen. I was enjoying the unknown; a traditionally foreign concept for me.

I reached into the white box and pulled out a fountain pen and a bottle of ink. I was pleasantly surprised. I had always wanted a fountain pen. I had been told that I have exceptionally neat handwriting. I carefully placed my new gifts on the table. I picked up my journal and handed it to Master Akio. "My friend Sara gave me all these things."

Master Akio carefully inspected both sides of the artwork on my journal, then stopped and asked, "Open?"

"Yes, of course."

Master Akio opened the book. When he saw the crisp white linen, his energy changed. Tears began to stream down his face as he took a long sniff of the paper and then squeezed the journal to his heart. He was hugging my journal with deep emotion. Even though it was my journal I took no offense, which was, truth be known, a complete and utter shock to me. I was not really a sharing kind of person. Yet somehow I knew that Master Akio was remembering something. I waited patiently.

Slowly, the tears stopped. Master Akio gradually opened his eyes and softly said, "Father make paper. Father best in Japan."

When Master Akio spoke about his father, I felt his pride in both his father and his country. Pride in a father was something I had never felt. My mood darkened. If I ever saw my father again…

Many times since I was a child I had dreamed of swinging a baseball bat at my father. He was on the ground, writhing in pain from my first blow to his head, and I wanted to hit him again and again. I blamed my father and family for a lot of my personal issues.

Master Akio brought me back to the moment as he described his father further. "Father make paper for Emperor. Emperor use only Father's paper." He paused, then added, "Before war, Akio make paper. War start, go to military school."

Master Akio unclenched my journal and handed it back to me. "Book have good paper."

I slowly took the journal from him. He smiled at me with one of his big, infectious smiles, then turned and went back to the dishes. He picked up a bowl and, slightly turning his head, asked me, "What Graham write?"

I smiled back at Master Akio. "My friend, Sara, gave me the book so I could write about my experiences on the island."

Master Akio nodded his head in approval. "Sara smart friend!" He refocused on the dishes, leaving me to the daunting task of writing my first journal entry.

I carefully opened the bottle of ink, filled the small reservoir in the pen, and took a couple practice strokes on the wrapping paper. The ink flowed smoothly. The pen was exceptionally well weighted. It felt wonderful in my hand. I was careful not to smudge the paper.

Now I was stuck. I didn't know what to write. I don't know how long I was lost in thought when I heard, "Graham... Graham.... Just start... Use date." I looked up to see Master Akio standing beside me, smiling as usual. "Graham, put date to start."

I dated the page August 28, 2010.

> I have been on the island for
> three days already. It has been
> the most incredible three days,
> yet, at the same time, it has been
> the worst three days of my life.
>
> Captain Taka had only just
> dropped me and my supplies off
> on the island when I had a full
> scale panic attack. Like what the
> hell was I thinking?

I felt a hand touch me on the shoulder and I jumped as if I didn't know who it was. Master Akio's touch brought me back to the island and my body. I'd been hunched over my journal for a very long time. My back hurt and my hand was cramped from writing for so long. I looked down at my journal and was shocked to discover I had written over ten pages. Ten pages! It was no wonder I hurt. I slowly looked around the camp. The sun had moved across the sky and it was now very late afternoon. How could I have been so lost in writing that I didn't notice?

Master Akio asked me, "Graham stop? Or more time need?" I looked at him and noticed he had found my mask and snorkel. He had also made himself a spear.

"I am done. I see you've been busy."

He blushed when I commented on him wearing the snorkel and mask. He sputtered, "Sorry not ask. Akio put back."

"No, Master Akio. My belongings are your belongings, too. Use what you need. We are sharing everything."

Master Akio grinned and said, "Thank you!" He added, "You say Master Akio."

"Yes, I know!" I stood up and started walking toward the ocean. "Are we talking or going fishing?"

Still grinning, Master Akio replied, "Fishing!" and then raced off towards the water.

It took us a long time to catch a couple of large fish. My spear fishing skills needed a lot of work, but Master Akio caught both fish quite easily. I almost caught a few, but, as with all great fishing tales, mine got away.

I carried the fish back to the kitchen just as rain started to fall. I slipped off my clothes, set them neatly in a pile, and ran to throw a couple dry logs on the fire in an attempt to keep it burning through the rain. I didn't really want to find out how good my wet firewood lighting skills were.

My experience with the rain yesterday made me guess it would rain really hard for about ten minutes and then stop. Quickly, I ran to the tent for my shampoo and shaving kit. I was well soaked from the warm tropical rain by the time I got back to the kitchen. I quickly put water on to heat before walking back into the rain to shampoo my hair and wash the salt off my body. I motioned for Master Akio to come over and yelled, "Master Akio, come wash your hair."

He quickly shed the clothes I'd given him and joined me in the rain. I put some shampoo in his hands and warned him not to get it in his eyes.

Master Akio was squeaky clean in a matter of minutes and was soon playfully dancing in the rain, enjoying the water splashing all over him. He danced for a while before returning to the shelter of our kitchen awning, sporting a huge, impish grin. It was becoming infectious. I couldn't help myself; when Master Akio was grinning I found myself grinning too.

The rain slowly diminished. I walked over and checked the temperature of the water on the stove. It felt just right. First, I set out two basins and then filled each with the warm water. I placed soap, a razor, and a face cloth beside each basin - one for Master Akio and one for me. I was really looking forward to having a shave as it had been three long, sweaty, hard days since my last. Master Akio had a few errant whiskers. I placed a mirror and shaving cream between the basins.

Master Akio's insatiable curiosity got the best of him and he wandered over to the basins to investigate what was going on. "Master Akio, the water is to wash and shave with," I said.

He looked deeply perplexed. "Shave?"

I chuckled. "Yes, a shave. To cut our whiskers. Our facial hair," I said as I patted my face. Then I picked up the closest razor and made the motions of shaving my face. I could clearly see that Master Akio didn't understand the concept of shaving at all. He appeared to be struggling with his words.

"Graham, Akio no shave."

I took the mirror to Master Akio and held it in front of his face. He cautiously took it from me. It took him a few seconds to get the mirror at the right height and angle for him to see his reflection. He recoiled in a mixture of shock and bewilderment. It was the first time he had seen a clear reflection of his face since the war – more than 60 years ago. He examined every inch of his face; every line and wrinkle that wasn't there the last time he used a mirror. Finally, with great effort, Master Akio said, "Inside Akio still young. Outside Akio old man. Much time pass since war."

I decided it best to give Master Akio some time with his thoughts. I went about washing my face and shaving. When I was almost through, I noticed he was watching me with a mixture of curiosity and fascination.

Master Akio made loud *Oohhhs* and *Aahhhs* as he applied the warm face cloth to his leathery face. He didn't need much shaving foam, as he only had a few whiskers on his chin, but he chose to plaster it on his entire face. With each stroke of the razor he examined his face in the mirror.

After he completed his shaving, there were more *Oohhhs* and *Aahhhs* as he washed his face one last time with warm water. When he was done, he turned and gave me a deep, crisp bow. As he rose he said, "Thank you, Graham. Today first shave!"

I merely smiled and said, "You're welcome."

I put all our toiletries back into the tent and rinsed out our basins. Master Akio hung the face cloths to dry. Now we were ready to start cooking supper!

Supper was an easy decision since we had just caught fish. Master Akio filleted the fish while the rice was cooking. I breaded the fish and then pan fried it in butter and onions. We made Earl Grey tea and ate while watching the sun set from the living room.

As the sun slowly sank on the horizon, so did my energy level. I was barely able to keep my eyes open as we washed our dishes in the dark. My arms felt like they weighed 80 pounds each. I could barely hold them up.

I said to Master Akio, "I am going to bed. Do you want the cot or the ground?"

"Ground."

I staggered off to the tent and threw a couple blankets on the ground for Master Akio. I collapsed with exhaustion onto the cot and sleep quickly overtook me. Master Akio washed the dishes and cleaned up before going to bed.

Days Four to Ten

For the next seven days it became our ritual to rise just before sunrise and meditate until the sun had risen well above us. Then I would run. Or attempt to. I did a lot of walking, but Master Akio would coax me to run all the way to the edge of the cove and back. He then led me in a series of stretches and exercises. We'd have a quick break before we practiced with our swords until my arms ached. They kept hurting for hours afterwards.

We followed sword practice with a quick swim in the ocean, then a hearty breakfast and cleanup of the entire camp. We also gathered and stacked more firewood, did our laundry, and swept out the tent.

After camp was clean we practiced with our swords again before breaking for lunch. After lunch I journaled while Master Akio had a short nap.

When he woke, we would go swimming and fishing in Sara's Cove. Master Akio always seemed to catch at least one fish. I was getting closer to spearing a fish every time out but had not been successful, yet.

Most afternoons it would rain, allowing us to wash ourselves. We finished our personal grooming with a shave. Finally, all clean, we'd cook supper and eat while watching the sun go down. We'd do our dishes and then I would collapse exhausted in bed waking the next morning to do it all over again.

Day Eleven

Master Akio woke me just before dawn as usual. Groggily, I stumbled out into the living room and sat down on the bench to meditate. The sky was just beginning to show its rosy morning colours. I closed my eyes and began to concentrate solely on my breathing as Master Akio had taught me. My only thought was on my breath in. Then I concentrated on my exhale. Breathe in, breathe out, breathe in, breathe out. I was peacefully relaxed, completely absorbed in my morning meditation when a picture materialized in my head.

I could see Master Akio sneaking up behind me with his wooden sword in hand. Stealthily, he crept towards me like a cat ready to pounce. He silently raised his sword over his head, poised and ready to strike. I could suddenly see the whole camp. I saw my sword off to my right. I also felt some deep-seated need to move and move now!

In a flash, I grabbed my sword and leapt forward, rolling onto my right shoulder and leaping into a standing position, all in one fluid motion. I stood alert, cautious and at the ready, my chest heaving from my extreme and sudden exertion. I waited for Master Akio's next move.

Master Akio smiled, but not his usual impish grin. It was a smile of acknowledgement and praise for a job well done. He bowed a deep, respectful bow and said, "Graham did good. Today not train. Body need rest."

I was shocked to discover that the whole scene was not just in my mind but had actually happened! My aching body was very happy to hear that there would be no training today. I think I even let out an audible, "Thank goodness!"

Master Akio said, "First breakfast, then long walk. Graham see Akio home." The idea of exploring and having an opportunity to see where Master Akio had spent the last 60-some years of his life got me very excited. I couldn't imagine the hardships he must have endured over the years.

It seemed to take forever to make breakfast and clean up. We packed a small knapsack with eight bottles of water, a snack, my GPS, and my journal, which Master Akio insisted I take. I thought this was really strange, but I did as I was asked. We made sure the fire was out and collected wood for our evening fire. We piled it under a tarp to keep it dry from the afternoon rains.

We were ready to go, or so I thought, when Master Akio pointed to my sword and said, "Take." He picked up both his practice sword and his real one. I was curious as he had not worn his real sword at all during the last seven days.

Master Akio made one final inspection of the camp area and then said, "Okay, we go," before starting in the direction of my crash site.

We were making good time compared to the last time I walked this route. It seemed like no time before we rounded the

Dog Leg and were heading north. The sound of the waves had a calming effect, and we were content to walk in silence.

We had walked a long way when Master Akio finally said, "Graham call Akio 'Master' many days. Akio teach Graham many things already. Graham good student."

He stopped abruptly and turned to face me. He looked into my eyes and asked, "Graham want learn all Akio know?" I opened my mouth to answer, but he held up his hand for me to wait. "Akio know only old ways and old things. Akio teach Graham about body temple, respect, love, discipline, and honour. Graham, want Akio teach you these things?"

He deliberately looked deep into my eyes and I felt his gaze pierce directly into my heart. I was compelled to answer. It seemed like just a moment ago I was standing on the top of a hill and now I was running; propelled forward with no choice. There was only one answer to give.

I looked directly into Master Akio's eyes and said, "Yes, I would like you to teach me."

He smiled. "Graham, student job very hard. Master no give answers. Master give student hard jobs. Master give student..." He struggled to find the right word. His posture and the tone of his voice changed, and he tried again, "Graham, listen. Master give student very hard job. Student job - do hard job, even when not understand or know why."

I had read a few books on the ancient quests and some history books on what the old Master/Student relationship was like. In the old days, no matter what the Master said the student did. No matter how ridiculous or unreasonable the Master's demands were, the student fulfilled them without question.

Despite this knowledge, and the apprehension about what might lay ahead if I were to choose this path, I still felt compelled to say, "Master Akio, I would be honoured for you to teach me." It was weird; it was like some giant force was operating my mouth. I felt my jaw moving and I heard my voice say yes. But it felt foreign. The old Graham had to be in complete control all the time. He would never blindly follow anyone, or willingly give up control. . . ever!

Master Akio smiled again and turned back up the beach. "We walk more." So, we walked on towards my old crash site.

After a few minutes, he stopped, looked into my eyes, and with a very serious tone in his voice said, "Graham, Master ask student three times. Student say "yes" three times, now bond. Only Master or death stop bond. Bond forever."

He stopped to let me consider his words. "Graham, think. Akio ask one time more. Graham say "yes", bond forever."

As his words sunk in, the old Graham exploded inside my head. *Are you fucking stupid?!? Run, Graham, run! You're too good for this crap! Don't listen to this crazy old man. You have a great life.* Yet, I stood silent.

The old inner voice changed tactics and began to bellow at me. *No one tells Graham Alexander Connelly what to do! Especially not some old, half-crazed man.*

I could feel the panic burst inside of me. *What the hell am I thinking? A life bond? No one said anything about a life bond!* I could feel my legs quiver and I began to hyperventilate.

Then from deep within me came a calming, peaceful voice of reason. *Graham, what do you really want? Recognize that the child-like voice of your mind is scared and doesn't even want you to think about this potential bond, let alone agree to it. Graham, feel into this. What does your heart want?*

In that moment of calmness, the clarity of my heart was heard for the first time. *Graham, your head is correct. It is scary and we don't know what to really expect, but the truth is that since you met Master Akio you have been more alive than ever before. In just a few days this man has taught you more about yourself than anyone. Graham, this is why you are on this island. You came back to find yourself and the Universe provided you Master Akio. Graham, you are to be Master Akio's student.*

Slowly my breathing returned to normal and I became conscious that I was walking on the beach with Master Akio once again. I was still puzzled though. My heart spoke the truth - I did come to find myself and I was doing just that. But what was this crap about the Universe giving me Master Akio? That part really confused me.

We walked in silence as I mulled over the concept of the Universe providing.

I broke the silence with a question. "We are almost at my old camp. When did you know we were camped there?"

Master Akio smiled, "When I hear big, noisy, flying bee. I follow noise, find camp, see men leave." I was puzzled; flying bee? Then it hit me. Master Akio had probably never seen a helicopter before.

A moment later a thousand questions leapt into my brain. "Why didn't you try to stop us from leaving? Why not light a fire, or signal us somehow?"

The almost permanent smile on Master Akio's face faded. "Akio not know war over. Not know who have big, noisy, flying bee. Not see Japanese or American flag. Akio hide, then ask, "War over?" Men go. Akio walk to site every day, hope men come back. One day, Graham come back. Akio find Graham, follow to camp."

I turned and asked Master Akio, "Where was your camp?" I noticed his impish smile creep across his face again. He merely said, "Not far" and continued walking.

We walked along the beach for another fifteen or twenty minutes, past the site where Blaine and I had camped after our crash. It seemed so casual to think of it as just a camp now. While Blaine and I were living in our lean-to, we had terrible visions of never being rescued, that Majuro Atoll had forgotten about us, or that our rescuers crashed in the thunderstorms. We imagined dying of hunger or thirst on this island. It was a horrific experience for both of us.

Yet walking along this same beach now, I was beginning to feel very comfortable on the island. Having Master Akio around helped a lot.

Master Akio veered off the beach and started walking towards the jungle. He wandered down what appeared to be a small game trail. We walked the path in silence for about ten minutes when Master Akio abruptly stopped, turned to me and said, "Welcome to my home." Then he turned and continued on down the path. I took about 30 steps and stopped, my mouth hanging open. I had stepped into a fairytale!

Before me, in a small clearing, was a perfect little Japanese homestead. It was a scene out of any of the hundred or so samurai movies I had watched on TV. I was amazed. I saw two buildings - one large and one smaller. Both had the perfect winged roof of historic Japanese architecture.

Master Akio turned and looked back at me. He saw the look on my face and said, "Graham surprised? Akio build many, many years. Need keep busy." With a mischievous tone, he added, "Not want get fat."

I smiled and replied, "Master Akio, I am surprised to see all this, but I am also in complete awe. I would never be able to build this, never mind create it so nicely."

Master Akio took me for a tour of his estate. We started in his incredibly well built, three room home. Everything was built with bamboo. The walls were made by placing bamboo tightly together vertically. The floor was also made from tightly placed bamboo covered in palm frond mats.

There was a small entryway where we took off our shoes. The main room was what I would call the living room and kitchen all in one. The house had a small bedroom off to the side, which had two or three grass mats piled together as a bed. The third room was actually larger than the other two combined. It was like an artist workshop and gallery. There were papers and what looked like paint brushes of various sizes, textures and shapes all over the place. The room was overflowing with them, yet they were all neatly stacked and piled together. It was like there was 10,000 square feet of paper packed into a 1,000 square foot room. It was mind boggling and yet amazing at the same time.

After Master Akio checked on various papers he had left to dry almost two weeks ago, he took me outside to his temple. I wasn't surprised when he asked me to take my shoes off before we entered his house, but it did surprise me to have to take my shoes off before we entered the compound of the temple.

The temple was a simple, raised platform with four-foot high walls made from palm fronds woven together. It was capped with a thatched, winged roof. Inside were various scrolls hanging along the walls and one large scroll hanging from the roof in the very center of the room. The ground beneath and around the temple was covered in sand and raked into a pattern. It was surrounded by a small fence. Master Akio had built his own Zen garden.

Curious, I asked Master Akio, "What does the scroll in the middle of the temple mean?"

He turned and looked into my eyes. "It mean faith. It reminder keep faith even when hard to do. Akio not understand why things happen, but Father taught me all things happen for reason. Wait and lessons come. Sometimes need wait long time, but lessons come."

He paused. "Talk more later. We go to garden now."

We walked to his garden and again I was stunned. It was huge. I now understood what kept him alive for all these years. But as I surveyed the garden, I became confused. I was pretty sure tomatoes and carrots were not native to the Marshall Islands. "How did you get tomatoes and carrots?" I asked.

"Akio gardener on Wotje Atoll during war. Leave Wotje Atoll, take seeds." Then with a stern voice Master Akio said, "Please, Graham not ask about war. Akio tell Graham later." He turned away and said, "Come."

He set out at a quick pace following another small trail. I had to hurry to catch up and keep up. A few twists and turns down the trail and we came to a pool. Not just a little pool, but a huge, stone-lined pool. After a closer look, I saw there were actually two pools. The first was a small, stone-lined pool with fresh spring water bubbling up that flowed into and filled the much larger one. I looked at Master Akio and playfully said, "You had to do something so you wouldn't get fat, right?"

He smiled and simply said, "Yes," then slipped out of his clothes and without hesitation jumped into the pool. I don't think Master Akio had time to resurface from his initial plunge before I was out of my clothes and cannon balling into the pool. The fresh water felt exhilarating. It also tasted much better than the ocean.

We must have frolicked and played in the pool for more than an hour. It was Master Akio who got out of the pool first and said, "Eat now." Who was I to argue? After all, we were talking about food. I scrambled out and shook myself off. I hastily put on my clothes and ran down the path after Master Akio.

We stopped briefly in the garden to pick lettuce, tomatoes, carrots, and a few beets. We carried our bounty up to the house. We removed our shoes outside before going in. Master Akio pointed to a small stool and said, "Graham sit. Today, Akio make meal."

Every time I got up to help, or even offered to help, I was excitedly told to go back and sit down. Master Akio even teased me with, "Bad student – no listen," grinning as he spoke.

When his meal preparations were complete, Master Akio said, "Akio not like eat in house. We eat by water."

We took our meal down to the pool and sat in the shade. Lunch was very simple - a delicious salad mixture of everything we harvested from the garden tossed together with a sprinkling of dried coconut and a splash of coconut milk as dressing. It was scrumptious. We ate our salad off large coconut shell plates with our fingers and used small coconut shells as cups. Every time we were thirsty we just walked over to the small pool and filled our coconut glasses with cool, refreshing spring water. Doing the dishes was easy. We scrubbed the coconut shells in the sand and then rinsed the plates and cups with water from the pool. We walked back up to the house to put the dishes away.

Master Akio then motioned with his head for me to follow him. "We go to temple."

We took off our shoes and socks before we entered the compound. Master Akio bowed as he entered the temple and motioned for me to do the same. "Graham, we bow to show respect to temple. Bow not needed, no! Bow Akio's way show respect for great mystery of Universe. Temple symbol of great mystery."

It occurred to me that this was twice in one day that the word 'universe' had been presented to me. I wanted to ask Master Akio what it meant, but his tone of voice told me I should listen and not ask questions right now.

Master Akio continued, "Graham, Akio build, destroy and build temple ten times. Each time Akio build better. Why?

Akio build temple – build skills. Be better person. Learn patience. Graham build things one time, think finish. No. Akio Master, make Graham build many times. Graham build many times same thing, make better person."

As Master Akio looked intently at me, the lines on his face visibly soften. I felt the energy in his demeanor change. I don't know how, I just know I did. He smiled a deep, warm smile and continued, "Graham, Akio afraid teach Graham. Akio not know Graham's world, not know what out there. Graham leave island one day. Akio no leave. Akio old man. No family. No home off island." There were small tears in Master Akio's eyes. "Graham first friend Akio have many years. No luck Akio drift to island, no luck island have fresh water, no luck Akio have garden seeds in pockets when leave Wojte Atoll, no luck Akio live long, no luck Graham crash on island and come back. Graham, it not luck, it destiny! Why? Akio not know why, just know. It destiny Graham and Akio meet."

He paused and seemed to penetrate my very soul with his piercing gaze. "Graham, Akio ask again. Graham want Akio teach?"

When he asked me this third and final time, I knew with absolute certainty I was going to say yes, although I didn't have a clue why. I looked at him, steadied my voice, and spoke. "I, too, am scared; my stomach is rolling in somersaults. I don't know what the future holds for either of us. But I do know this with certainty - I want you to teach me what you know."

Master Akio's face was beaming with excitement and tears of joy started streamed down his face. He looked at me and said, "Akio accept Graham as student."

Another padlock on my soul clicked open and the doors swung a little wider. It was a weird feeling, yet I felt completely at peace. It was like the feeling I got after a long day of flying when heading on vacation. After spending the day in airport line-ups, dealing with foreign border agents, crazy taxi rides, getting into my room, changing my clothes, and finally sitting on the patio with a cold drink. The feeling I get knowing that I have arrived; that after all of the crazy and zany effort, it was all worth it.

Master Akio looked at me and said, "Graham, we find place for temple for Graham."

"My own temple?" I said.

Master Akio nodded, got up and walked towards the gate of the compound. "Yes, Graham need temple," he said.

I got up and followed. I smiled as I realized I didn't have a choice in the matter. What the master says, the student does without question.

We tromped all around the jungle behind Master Akio's temple for over an hour trying to find the perfect location for my temple. We needed a spot where I would not have to cut down any trees but could use the existing ones as supports. I would be permitted to cut down the grasses and scrub brush to clear the land, but no trees. I also needed a clear view to the east and the west. I must not to be able to see any building or man-made structure from the temple, only the raw, pristine jungle.

Once we found the perfect spot Master Akio pulled out his sword and cut four large handfuls of long grass. He found a small clearing and sat down, motioning for me to join him. He then spent the better part of an hour teaching me to braid grass into small lengths of rope.

My strands of rope were as tight as Master Akio's but they did not look like rope. I held up my creation and showed him, "Not bad for my first attempt, huh?"

"Yes, good for first time," he said as he examined my work. "Tie rope around four trees of new temple. That way Graham find temple spot when time to build."

I tied the newly made ropes at shoulder height around the four trees we selected as the pillars of my new temple. It felt weird to be thinking that I, Graham Alexander Connelly, would be building a temple. I'm sure just mentioning that to Sara or Blaine would get me strange looks. They would think I was completely off my rocker.

Master Akio said, "Akio work paper. Graham sit in temple place and journal." I had wondered why Master Akio made me bring my journal. I sat down in the middle of my four pillar trees, pulled out my journal, carefully placed the bottle of ink on the ground as to not spill any, and proceeded to write.

I was startled out of my reflections by Master Akio. "Graham, time we go. We need go to Graham's camp. We come here other day."

"Go? Why are we going back already? Didn't we just get here?"

Master Akio calmly replied, "Much to do at Graham's camp. We come back here later."

"What do we have to do back at the other camp, Master Akio?"

His face shone brightly with a teasing expression. "Graham, this joy of being Master. Master ask, student do."

I know the old Graham would have been furious with that playful but glib answer, but the new Graham realized this was all part of the training. I was to learn to trust and do what was asked of me without too much fuss. A mischievous grin spread slowly across my face as I bowed to him and said, "Yes, Master Akio, whatever you say."

"Graham finally good student - not argue all time!" he chuckled. "We must go now or we walk home in rain for long way."

We had only walked a little ways down the path when Master Akio turned to look back at his home. He paused. Smiling for a few brief moments, he then turned and continued walking to our shared camp.

I was puzzled, "Master Akio, we can call my camp the beach or Summer House, but what can we call your house?"

Master Akio turned and faced me, "Graham ask many questions. This one good question." He paused to consider for a moment, then declared, "Old House and Summer House."

We hurried towards our Summer House, trying to beat the daily rains. The first drops of the afternoon were upon us even before we made the Dog Leg. We were going to get very wet. I turned to Master Akio and said, "I thought you said we weren't going to get rained on."

He grinned, "No, Akio say we go soon or walk in rain for long time. Now we only walk in rain for short time!" I was glad I had placed my journal in a plastic bag prior to leaving the Old House.

By the time we had arrived at the Summer House the rain had stopped, but we were completely and utterly soaked. I gathered our face washing and shaving supplies, as well as some dry clothes for each of us. After a wash, a shave, and a change, life felt pretty good again.

It didn't take us long to whip up a hearty meal of spaghetti, meat sauce, canned peas, and some warm, freshly-baked-over-the-fire biscuits. We followed it with tea and coffee. The sunset was the perfect view for our feast.

Master Akio turned and faced me, "Graham, there is beer? Akio like one beer. Story telling good with beer."

"Story telling?"

"Yes."

I took our mugs and plates to the kitchen and went to the beer cooler. I lifted the lid and quickly counted our supplies. I called out, "Master Akio, we have six beers left." I grabbed two and walked back to the living room.

I handed Master Akio one and sat down. I heard the familiar *psssttt* as the cap was twisted off. Master Akio raised his bottle in salute to the ocean, "Cheers!" Then he turned and tapped our bottles together and raised his bottle to me in a salute, "Cheers!"

I opened my bottle of beer and repeated the whole process.

We both sat in silence for a long time before Master Akio spoke. "Graham, Akio want tell story how Akio come here. Then Graham please remember. Write down story so Graham know story."

I looked at Master Akio and nodded, "I will listen very carefully so I can make notes tomorrow."

He smiled, "Good." He turned his attention back to the ocean.

When Master Akio started speaking, his voice trembled slightly. "Akio make paper. In Washi all men in family make paper. During war, Father send Akio to Navy school to be officer, learn use radar. Akio also gardener on Wotje Atoll. Need gardener - Japan not send food for everyone." He paused for a brief moment. "Akio had orders tell Captain Shinichi

100

Yoshimi when see American planes and ships on radar, so we tell other islands. One night, Akio not sleep, walk on beach. Akio hear shells. Sudden big explosion!" He took a deep breath.

"Akio wake up on beach. Radar building destroy. Fire and explosion everywhere! Akio not hear them, only see them. Akio hear nothing." He shook his head. "Never see war like that. So much dead. Buildings on fire. Shells keep coming and coming. No place to hide. One more shell explosion - I fly twenty feet!"

I was on the edge of my seat, waiting for him to continue.

"Akio wake up. It night. Akio walk in dark to find Captain Shinichi Yoshimi. Command post destroy. Captain Shinichi Yoshimi body cut," he ran his hand across his waist.

"Akio look one or two hour, find no one alive. All men, all commanding officer dead. Many, many people in village dead." He shook his head sadly. "Akio lose many friends that night. Akio think it duty die also. Akio think seppuku." He made a motion of stabbing himself and running the sword back and forth across his middle. I knew from what I'd read that seppuku was ritual suicide and it was considered an honourable death amongst warriors.

"Akio hear voice say, "Akio, no seppuku. Akio tell other islands. Americans not land, they drop shell on islands.

This not how Americans fight war before. Americans change war. Japan must change also. Akio must tell other islands."

"Akio listen to voice, want tell other islands, but radio broke. Akio must go to other islands. Find boat. Put guns, food, water, medicine, and map in boat. Think other islands need food, so bring garden tools and seeds. Akio want go to Erikub Atoll to tell about new American war"

"Akio push boat off island. Want paddle to Erikub Atoll. Akio sleep, wake, paddle, sleep, wake, paddle all night. Wake up, it daylight. No see islands. Drift many days – maybe ten days and nights. One day, drift to this island."

Again he paused to take a deep breath. "Akio think many times seppuku, but voice say, "No! Not right time." Same voice tell Akio where find water on island, when go gather turtle eggs and bird eggs. Same voice tell Akio what to eat and not eat. Same voice tell Akio to exercise and practice sword every day."

He stared out at the ocean for a moment. "Many days and nights on beach Akio look for ships. Then storms come. Akio go into jungle to get out of storms. Go back to beach, look for ships less and less. Build house, temple, and pool. Many years Akio build, destroy, build. Build house and temple ten times. Now good!"

I stared at Master Akio and quietly waited for him to finish. There had to be more to the story. Slowly, he turned his head and looked at me. "Graham, Akio train for one year to use radar, shoot guns, be soldier. War come, but no use guns. War kill all friends. Akio hate Americans for kill all friends like this. No honour to kill with shells. Akio spend many years planning revenge on America."

Slowly, a small smile crept onto Master Akio's face. "But Akio lose need to kill. Akio forget revenge. Akio forgive. Forgive America for kill with no honour. Forgive Akio for want revenge."

I spoke quietly, looking him directly in the eyes, "It took many years for America to forgive Japan for bombing Pearl Harbor, but we did. I am told time heals all wounds."

We sat in silence for a moment. I took the last swallow from my beer. I stood up and asked Master Akio if he would like another beer. He nodded yes.

I walked back to the coolers and got us each another beer. That left us one beer each for my going away celebration. The thought flashed through my head that that was only eighteen days away. How could I learn all I needed to in only eighteen days?

I dropped our empties in the recycling bag and returned to Master Akio.

We both went through our honouring, beer-drinking salute. I chuckled at the simple ritual and wondered if I would continue it when I got home.

Master Akio turned towards me. "Graham, why you crash plane and why you come back here?" I looked at Master Akio and said, "Stupidity and arrogance."

He looked puzzled for a moment then laughed, "Akio has this also. Graham, what happen?"

I took a swig of my liquid courage. Honesty was hard. "We crashed because I terrorized my co-pilot." I sighed and explained. "I miscalculated the necessary fuel needed for the flight from Hawaii to Majuro Atoll. Normally, it is the co-pilot's job to check the calculations, but because he was very much afraid of me, he didn't. So we simply ran out of fuel. We lost a million dollar plane because of my arrogance."

Master Akio interrupted me, "Million dollar plane? That is much money?"

I replied, "Yes, it's a lot of money. We crashed the plane and then walked through the eight or ten smaller islands to this big one. We carried as many supplies as we could and made camp - the camp you cleaned up after we left. We were on the island for three days before we were rescued. We were flown to the Majuro hospital. We were extremely lucky we were in as good a shape as we were, we didn't find water or food as you did. The local police wanted to talk with us about the crash, so it took another day before we could fly home."

"Why Graham come back here?"

"I've been asking myself that. I have no idea other than it felt like I needed to. It was like some force was compelling me to do this. I needed to come here to find out who I am."

"Graham have name for this force?" I paused for a moment, reflecting on the question. "Actually, I don't."

Master Akio smiled, "Akio name it Universe."

Excitedly I asked, "Master Akio, this is the third time today I have heard the term 'The Universe'. What do you mean when you say 'The Universe'?"

"Same force bring Graham here, Akio name Universe. Force have many names. All names have same meaning. Some name it Buddha. Some say Nature, or Great Mystery. Some say God, The Force, Old Man, or Divine Presence."

Master Akio appeared to be lost in thought for a few moments. Finally, he spoke, "Look at sky, Graham. Universe have no limit, Universe always grow. Universe have many mysteries. Universe is energy. Universe use energy to create what it need. Universe give energy to Akio and to Graham to create."

He paused for a moment and continued. "Universe is all possibility. Universe is complete. Universe is for all. Universe and all other names, same intention - all men connected; all men depend on each other. If no Student, no Master. If no Master, no Student."

Akio searched my face to see if I understood. He added, "Graham, all things perfect. All things like temple."

I sort of understood, but I thought I should get some clarification. "So, the Universe is a way of being or a set of beliefs you hold?"

A smile flashed across Master Akio's face, "Graham, sometimes small knowledge is good idea. It starts mind to work. You need to figure out this question on your own. I help, but you have answers inside of you."

Master Akio stood. "Graham, Akio now go to bed. We train tomorrow." As soon as I heard the word 'train' I decided that it was a good time for me to go to bed as well. We dropped off our bottles in the recycling bag and went to the tent.

Day Twelve

We were back to the old routine. We woke up before the sun rose to meditate. After meditating, I ran to the Dog Leg and back. I still had to walk parts of the run, but those distances were getting shorter each day. Then we did our morning stretches.

Our morning exercises finished with sword practice. I liked this the most, but my shoulders didn't. They ached almost non-stop. *What I wouldn't give right now to have a back massage.*

We ended the usual morning workout with a quick swim - more shoulder and leg exercise.

After our now routine breakfast of porridge and canned fruit, our schedule changed abruptly. Normally, we would have had a small rest and then gone back to practicing with our swords. Today, Master Akio said, "Graham, Summer Home need temple. Graham need learn build temple before we build temple at Old House. We look for place. Bring axe and saw."

I was about to say something, but thought better of it. I shrugged my shoulders and went to get the axe, saw, and, as an added tool, the machete. I returned to Master Akio's side with the necessary tools.

He looked at me, "Summer House is Graham's - Graham choose - what side want temple?" I pointed to the

108

right, the opposite direction from the Dog Leg, a direction we didn't normally travel. He grinned, "Good choose."

We walked a fair ways up the beach before Master Akio turned and put his back to the jungle, facing the water. "Graham, what think Akio do?"

I walked over and stood next to Master Akio. I looked left, right, and then straight ahead. "You are making sure that we cannot see camp – our Summer Home - from here."

Master Akio smiled the smile I had come to love. It said he was pleased with my answer. He congratulated me. "Good answer! You correct!"

I was surprised for a moment. Not surprised by his praise, or by the fact that I was right, but by his use of the word 'you'. I realized that this was the first time I had ever heard him say 'you' instead of my name. I smiled. *I guess the Master is learning from the student as much as the student is learning from the Master.*

We turned and walked into the jungle. It took us over two hours of walking back and forth, sitting down amongst the palm trees, walking to another area, and sitting down again before we both agreed on the exact location and size of our new temple. Once we decided on the location, Master Akio cut four large handfuls of long grass. Returning with the grass, he sat down cross-legged in the middle of our new temple area and invited me to join him. Together we braided the grass into small ropes. I still struggled with my braiding, but I was enjoying it far more today than when I first learned the process.

When the ropes were all braided, Master Akio got up and said, "Graham, we start temple today. We must make offering to Universe - say thank you for giving so much."

"What's an offering?" I asked.

Master Akio smiled. "Offering is small gift and blessing. Something you make. Something from you heart."

I told him I would think about what the offering would be as we tied the grass ropes to each of the four support trees.

Master Akio stood back to look at our newly marked temple location and said to me, "We go make offering now. We not start make temple before make offering." He turned to look intensely into my eyes. "Akio not help. Graham make offering." He paused, ensuring I understood the seriousness of this task, then continued, "Graham, offering very important. Make offering from heart. Make good offering."

I was stumped. Besides my sword and the meals, I hadn't made anything since I arrived. I told Master Akio I needed some time to reflect on this. We walked back to camp in silence. I was struggling to come up with even one idea for an offering when *WHAM;* I felt like I'd been hit between the eyes. I was going to carefully take a page out of my journal and write on it as my offering. My journal had become very sacred to me over the last few days and Master Akio said the paper was of very good quality. I was very pleased with this idea. It seemed like the perfect gift.

I scurried off to the tent and came back with my journal. I scrounged around in the storage containers looking for a very sharp knife. I quickly found a paring knife and took it to the kitchen table with my journal. I laid the book flat then carefully cut a page out. It actually felt somewhat sacrilegious to cut my sacred tome.

The old Graham would be laughing at my affinity for a stupid little book in which one writes their experiences and feelings. I smiled at how far I'd come in such a short time. Then I laughed out loud when I realized that I was going to have to ask Sara where she bought the journal. I would need another as this one would be full before I left the island.

I picked up my journal, the loose page, and my pen and ink. Taking a bottle of water with me, I walked over to the living room and sat down. Now that I had the page, I needed to write something on it. Something wise, something profound; maybe a famous quote or some poetry.

Oh gosh, Graham, who are you kidding!?! You don't know any poetry or a famous quote. I opened the bottle of ink, dipped my pen in, then paused…

To the Universe,

I don't fully understand you yet. I know you have placed Master Akio in my life. I know you have

111

*given me a past; why that past I
don't know. I also don't know
what my future holds, but I am
open to having it unfold before
me and with me.*

I am open to you.

*Signed,
Graham Alexander Connelly*

I put the lid back on the ink and carefully capped my pen. I returned my journaling materials and my note to the Universe to the tent and went in search of Master Akio.

I stepped out of the tent and was immediately compelled to duck and swerve to my right. My abrupt and sudden movement saved me by mere milliseconds! Master Akio had thrown a coconut at my head as hard as he could and was now bearing down on me with his wooden sword drawn and at the ready. I quickly surveyed the surrounding area as I hastily drew my practice sword to meet Master Akio's charge. He had selected his ambush site very skillfully; it was definitely to my disadvantage. I was on the uneven, lower, and unquestionably rougher ground. He was on higher and much flatter ground. I kept scanning my surroundings, when fate smiled on me slightly. In my peripheral vision, I spied a small coconut on the ground to my right. I moved my stance slightly, my foot touching the coconut.

My sword still at the ready, Master Akio moved in and swung at me, trying to take my head off. *Holy Crap! He swung hard.* I parried his swing, my hands stinging slightly from absorbing the blow, and then I sprang into action. I scooped my foot under the small coconut and with a quick flick; I kicked the coconut at Master Akio.

With the amazing speed, agility, and grace of a gazelle, Master Akio deflected the coconut harmlessly over his left shoulder with his sword. He smiled that approving smile of his, but I didn't take any time to gloat. As he was momentarily distracted by the coconut, I promptly moved to take over the high ground. Master Akio's approving smile was now a grin that spread from ear to ear. I could only surmise that I had performed really well.

My location wasn't the only thing that suddenly changed. Master Akio's strokes became much faster, and far more furious. I was barely managing to parry or dodge his blows. *Graham Alexander Connelly, you are in serious trouble!* I had to figure out the changes in Master Akio's fighting style or I was going to get hit and hit hard - very soon! Then I saw it. It was just a subtle change in the way he was gripping his sword. Master Akio had moved both hands closer to the guard.   Frantically I parried up high, then, releasing my grip slightly, I slid both hands higher towards the guard to match Master Akio's grip. My strokes were now minutely faster, but that was all it took. Because I had higher and more level ground, the advantage was slightly leaning in my favour.

At this stage in my training, I took all the advantages I could get!

We soon fell into a rhythm - high swing to the left, high swing to the right, slash across the waist, high swing to the left, high swing to the right, slash across the waist. I knew at some level that Master Akio was testing me, trying to see what, if any, crazy risk I would take, or whether the rhythm of our strokes would cause me to lower my guard and present an opening. My job was to stay focused on the fight at hand, not give Master Akio any opening, and at the same time look for any potential openings to use against him.

I raised my sword high as a small, subtle opening in Master Akio's defenses presented itself. I was ready to strike down and across the body when a calm yet commanding voice told me, *No. Graham, stop.* I paused mid-stroke, almost breaking my wrist to halt my strike. As I stopped, Master Akio slipped on the uneven ground, dropping his guard. I wildly threw my sword off to one side, desperately grabbing out for him before he fell completely. He reached for my outstretched arm, steadying himself. We both stood there panting, out of breath, wild-eyed in the realization of what had just happened and what could have.

Master Akio slowly let go of my arm and looked directly at me. "Graham, how you know stop?"

I shook my head. "I don't know. A voice told me to stop." He looked at me, tears coursing down his face. "Graham, you good student. You use coconut to get high ground, then you take high ground. You see Akio strike faster and you learn how Akio do this. Even in battle you do this. Maybe fatal, but still you do. Then voice tell you do something and even in fight, you do it. Graham, you *great* student!"

A huge lump formed in my throat, almost making it impossible for me to swallow. No one had ever said I was great at anything. My eyes welled up. Tears began to slowly trickle down my cheeks. I could barely muster a heartfelt, "Thank you!" Master Akio looked at me and smiled. "Akio okay, just need sit."

I smiled, wiping away my tears. "Master Akio, you go sit down and I'll bring us some water." Master Akio went to rest in the living room while I went for water. I made sure to keep a watchful eye on him. I was going soft. I had never felt this protective of someone else's health and well-being. This island was doing weird things to me.

I closed the lid on the cooler and walked back to the living room. I suddenly realized that as I got into better shape I would have to be a little more careful when sparring with Master Akio - he must be well over 80 years old.

I handed Master Akio a bottle of water and sat down on the bench next to him. He offered a sincere and gracious, "Thank You!"

I took a few precious moments to gaze out at the blue-green water. I made a mental note - invariably it was going to rain later today. It rained every afternoon. I turned and asked, "Master Akio, how old are you?"

He grinned, "Akio not know. Not know year now!" I shook my head, awed by the profound realization that Master Akio had no calendar for the last 60 or so years! He would have relatively no noticeable passage of the seasons here in the middle of the Pacific Ocean. So, he really could have no clue about the passing of time. That was such an odd idea to me.

Master Akio grinned. "You add years. Akio born 1920." When I finished mentally calculating his age my jaw actually dropped. I stared at Master Akio. He was 90 years old!

"Master Akio, you're 90 years old!" I squealed excitedly. He cocked his head to the side and asked, "That is old?"

I smiled and reached over to put my arm on his shoulder and shake it gently, "Oh yes, it is!"

Master Akio stood. He had a silly grin on his face. I knew he was going to say something to try to rouse a response out of me. He crossed his arms and tried his best to look serious, "So, Graham, you like lose to old man in sword fight?"

I slowly stood up, trying my best to look mean and menacing. I scowled at him and, using my toughest voice, asked, "Who said I lost?" We stood there staring at each other, both trying our best to look more intimidating than the other.

We lasted about 30 seconds before we both broke into peals of laughter. It crossed my mind that I had laughed more

116

in the last twelve days than in all the years leading up to this adventure.

I put my hand back on Master Akio's shoulder and said, "I think it's lunch time. What do you think?"

He nodded in agreement. "Yes to lunch! You have offering?"

"Yes, I have an offering for the temple."

"You good student, no matter what Blaine think."

"No matter what Blaine thinks? He's not even on the island, so it really doesn't matter what he thinks!"

"Akio see if Graham get angry," he smiled as he spoke. "You must learn not be angry so fast."

The old Graham would have been furious and probably would have pouted for a week over this. Now, I simply heard what he said and considered it something to focus on. I was amazed at myself and how far I had come in these ten days with Master Akio.

After a quick and simple meal, Master Akio dried the lunch dishes. He was hanging up the dish towel when he looked towards me. I had just finished putting half a dozen bottles of water in my backpack along with my offering for the temple. He said, "We need take axe, saw, and rope."

I nodded in agreement, "I already have them, Master Akio."

He nodded his head in appreciation, "Good, Graham."

117

I was all set. I had my backpack and our tools. We had water and my special offering for the temple. I threw on the backpack and we marched down the beach towards the new temple site. I was both excited and nervous; I had never really built anything, especially not something as significant as a temple.

We had walked about 50 yards down the beach when Master Akio said, "Graham, we have much work to do."

"I am not afraid of doing real work and lots of it, Master Akio."

He stopped and turned to look towards me. He had a very serious expression on his face. "Akio know you work hard, Graham. You show me you train very hard, every day. Not worry if you work hard. Build temple is more than hard work. Even when you not want work, you work with love. Everything you do to build temple, you must put love in. You must love work, you must love trees, grasses, even the leaves you build with, you must love what temple stand for."

Before I could ask him what he meant, he continued, "Graham, we are energy. Energy all around us. Energy grow energy. You want more love in you life, you must give more love. Understand, Graham?"

I looked him in the eyes. "I think so. I think you're saying that people can feel energy in things, like the things we make. When things are made with love, by people who love to

118

create them, then we feel the love in those things. So, things made with love are better?" I asked.

Master Akio didn't answer, but his expanding grin spoke volumes. I suddenly understood so many things. I slapped my forehead. "I get it! Sarah's cooking and baking always tastes so good because her secret ingredient is love."

"You start understand, Graham. All things love, all things sacred, all things like temple, all things come from Earth and Universe."

I nodded my head vigorously in agreement. I think I really was starting to understand.

Satisfied, Master Akio turned and started heading back down the beach towards our new temple site. I fell into step beside him. We were starting out fairly late in the day, so I was unsure of how much we would actually get done today. As we got closer and closer to the site, I became more and more excited about the upcoming adventure. We continued to walk in silence along the hot, sandy beach. We stopped just before the new temple site, dropping all our tools and my backpack in the soft sand.

Master Akio looked at me, "Graham, we sit here and meditate. Bring your offering and meditate with it."

I rummaged through the backpack and found my temple offering. Carefully, I took the folded piece of paper out and followed Master Akio a little closer to the ocean. He motioned for me to sit in the sand next to him, facing the crystal blue

119

waters. For a moment all we could hear was the sound of the waves crashing on to the beach.

"We meditate and give thanks to five elements: air/wind, water, sky/heaven, fire, and earth. Graham, in this meditation, you give thanks. Ask for blessing for temple from five elements."

"Is this a silent meditation or can I use words?"

"You decide. Do what heart feels right."

I wrinkled my nose slightly, "But I don't know what feels right. I have never done this before."

Even before the smile lines on Master Akio's face softened, I could feel the subtle shift in his energy. "Graham, what you do for meditation, for blessing, is perfect." He looked deeper into my eyes. "Graham, Akio throw coconut at you, but you know move and coconut not hit you. You think not know what do for offering, but you find offering in heart. Same place - you know move, you know offering - now you know what do for meditation and blessing."

My nose was still wrinkled ever so slightly; I was truly uncomfortable with what Master Akio was asking me to do. It was one thing to dodge a coconut; it was an entirely different thing to trust some unknown source with my words and my actions. I had spent my whole life believing that I was my thoughts.

Rather reluctantly and very slowly, I closed my eyes. I began to concentrate on nothing but my breathing. As I focused on how the air moved through my nose and filled me, the sound of the ocean waves gradually faded. I could feel my chest rise and fall in a rhythmic pattern. With each breath, the heaviness in my body began to diminish. Soon it felt like my physical body was nothing more than air. I could no longer distinguish between my body and the world around me; we were composed of the same material. We were one.

At the sheer thought of being one with the air, the old Graham reared his ugly head. *What the Hell are you thinking? What do you think you're doing? Every rational, sane person knows that you can't be one with the wind. Why are you entertaining this crazy, old man's ideas? He's been trapped all alone, on a deserted island for almost 70 years. He probably has dementia or something; he definitely has a few screws loose. The guy's nice enough, but come on; this is pretty crazy stuff he's talking about!*

I laughed to myself. Was this what a schizophrenic felt like - having conversations in their head, multiple voices talking like you did not even exist? I smiled as I recognized that the voice of the old Graham was nothing more than what Sara called my ego. Ego was the small child that always wanted my attention.

My smile grew as I recognized and understood what the old Graham stood for and why my ego was responding the way it was. The old Graham only believed in what he could see, feel, touch, and of course, control.

Once again I focused on my breath; my chest rising and falling with each rhythmic inhale and exhale. Slowly, the sensation of my body as one with the wind swept over me again.

Gently, I felt my consciousness drawn towards the rhythmic sound of ocean waves crashing upon the beach. The sound became louder and louder. Physical sensation - like the sweltering tropical heat - returned to my body. I could feel the perspiration on my face and beads of sweat running down the small of my back. Despite the physical discomforts, I felt invigorated and at peace.

I sensed Master Akio had not yet finished his meditation. I gingerly opened my eyes to gaze out at the beautiful blue ocean while I waited patiently. It only seemed like a very few moments when I sensed Master Akio starting to move next to me.

As Master Akio stood up, he carefully turned to face me and give me one of his consume-the-whole-face smiles. Slowly and carefully, I dusted the sand off my legs as I stood. My recent meditation had left me with a feeling of peacefulness and mindfulness. I felt there was no real need to rush to do anything.

Starting from my left side, I scanned the horizon to take in the magnificent scenery of the beach. I slowly shuffled my feet to turn towards the jungle, taking in the sheer splendor. I shuffled my feet again as I continued turning, now looking towards our camp –the Summer Home. A contented sigh escaped from my lips.

I spotted my backpack a few feet away and realized how thirsty I was. I took a bottle of water and offered Master Akio one as well. He graciously accepted it with a slight bow and a nod of his head. Almost in unison, we twisted the caps off the bottles, took big mouthfuls of water, and then replaced the caps. Together, we turned to look directly at our new temple site.

"Graham, what you bring as offering?" Master Akio asked without looking at me.

"A piece of paper from my journal. I wrote something on it."

"So how you want offer your paper to temple? You want hang in temple? You want bury in ground beneath temple? You want light fire and burn paper as offering?"

I thought for a few moments before I replied. "I didn't know I had options. But if I do, then I would like to hang my offering in the temple."

"Graham, Akio not know what you write, but Akio like idea see many times your first words of wisdom."

"So, Master Akio, what is your offering?" I asked excitedly.

"I think long time. I think maybe give paper and make scroll from home, but have scrolls in my temple. Want this be our temple. I decide give sword we make to hang in temple."

I made an audible gasp, "But, how are we going to train if you don't have a sword?"

Master Akio turned towards me with a very serious look on his face. "Graham, jungle there full of trees. We make other sword. That bad sword. It make Akio slip and almost fall."

I grinned and then teased Master Akio, "A bad sword? I was told a good craftsman never blames his tools."

Master Akio smiled, "Yes! It good sword. Have many good memories so far. This why I want hang in our temple. Sword symbol of new beginning and deep friendship."

I looked into the jungle where the new temple was going to be built. "Master Akio, I like that we are both hanging something inside our new temple."

"Akio like also. Graham, we start work now. Time to build temple."

I nodded in agreement and walked over to our tools. I picked them up and walked towards the jungle. *It's about darn time we get to actually build this thing!*

We both walked the short distance into the jungle. Master Akio stopped to turn towards me. "We do messy work outside of temple area. Not much saw and hammer near temple. We measure in temple, go out to cut. Bring cut wood to temple to put in right place."

"Makes sense to me."

Master Akio picked up the saw, the axe, and the hatchet. "First we give thanks for our tools." He held up the tools and offered a prayer to the Universe. "We give thanks for our tools. We give thanks for tools make work more easy. We give thanks to all people we see and not see who make tools. Thank you!"

Master Akio then explained to me that we need to place our offerings inside of our temple today and each day after this. By leaving our offerings in the middle of the temple site, as we built the temple around them they would become part of the energy of the place.

"Graham, Akio build Old Temple and Old House for many years. I use many different blessings and traditions. I not have years to teach you all traditions. We use new blessings for our temple. We make new traditions. You take home blessings and new traditions."

Master Akio assigned me my first task. "Graham job now cut many, many trees, but first put hand on every tree and say thank you to tree."

Master Akio could see the puzzled look on my face so he continued. "We all energy, trees all energy. Cut tree – tree no more tree energy, now board energy. Trees not live, now new energy for board. We say thank you to trees."

I wasn't sure if I perfectly understood what he was saying, but I didn't think it would hurt to try it anyway. "What size of trees and how many would you like?" I asked.

He asked me to follow him and we walked a little deeper into the jungle. He stopped and touched a tree. "We want twenty this tree." He walked to another size of tree and said, "We want 40 this tree." He continued to walk and touch different trees, offering instructions. "We want ten this tree. We want more than forty 40 this tree. Graham not take all trees from one area; take from big area at good walk away from temple."

I let out a slight groan. I knew what my job for the next few days was going to be. Chop a tree, haul a tree, chop another tree and haul another tree. When that was done, I would have to chop down and haul even more trees.

I turned to Master Akio. "Can you tell I just figured out what my job is going to be for the next few days?"
He replied, "Akio job weave mats from leaves of trees you cut. Please cut palm tree now so I start weave now."

After chopping down my fifth palm tree of the day, I concluded that palm trees are a very hard wood. With each stroke of the axe I found myself fantasizing about a chainsaw. I don't know if Master Akio would approve of me using a chainsaw, but it sure would make this part of the job much easier.

After I finished hauling and stacking the fifth tree, Master Akio looked at me with a satisfied look and said, "I think time for fish, wash, and cook."

I could not have agreed more whole-heartedly! I walked over and looked at the pile of palm fronds that Master Akio had amassed from the palm trees I brought him. It was quite the huge pile. I also noticed that Master Akio had been sitting on the ground while weaving the mats together. I decided that tomorrow I would build him a small bench and maybe a table to work on. We gathered up the backpack, our water bottles, and the tools and started back towards the Summer House.

After a quick sip of water, we were off to the ocean to catch our supper. I wasn't much of a fisherman back home in Hawaii, but I sure enjoyed going out every day on this island. It didn't take Master Akio long before he had a couple of nice sized fish. Even though I'd brought many cans of chicken and turkey to eat, it just seemed to be the right thing to do while living on an island - catch supper out of the ocean.

Although we had doubled the number of mouths being fed from my food supplies, there was very little chance of us running out. I had brought enough to double my stay. I chuckled, "What was I thinking?"

I was about to start the cooking when Master Akio shooed me out of the kitchen and told me to go write in my journal. This was the first supper that he was going to cook for us. He had made lunches on his own before, but never supper. I was a bit reluctant, especially because I love to cook. I eventually agreed to let Master Akio prepare our meal, but not before I got the coffee and the water boiling for tea.

It only took me a few minutes to retrieve my journal from my backpack and grab a cup of freshly made coffee before I settled down to write. I decided to stay at the kitchen table as we had not yet had our daily rain and the clouds were building. No sooner had I put pen to paper than I heard the familiar splat of the rain on the awning. In less than fifteen seconds, the sky opened up and we were once again experiencing a Pacific Ocean downpour. The good thing about the rainstorms on this island was that in less than half an hour they were completely over.

Just as the rain stopped, Master Akio told me that supper was ready. Reluctantly, I put my pen down and closed my journal, being careful to safely tuck it back into the plastic bag in my backpack. My journaling would have to wait until tomorrow.

With great curiosity, I wandered over to the cooking area to see what culinary masterpiece Master Akio had created for us. As I got closer, I couldn't tell exactly what spices he used but it smelled simply divine.

When I reached the stove I could see that tonight's delectable feast was fish smothered in sautéed onions, with a side of buttered pasta garnished with stewed tomatoes. It looked and smelled good!

Carefully, I carried our plates of food out to our living room. I made a second trip for a couple bottles of water before settling in to watch another magnificent sunset.

When I get back to Hawaii I'm going to have to look at getting a place that has an unobstructed view of the ocean so that I can see the sunset every night. I chuckled to myself. It would be pretty cool to have Sara and Blaine over to my new place, wherever it is, for a glass a wine or a couple beers and just to watch the sun go down. *Gawd! I'm getting soft-hearted.*

Master Akio and I quickly settled into our respective seats, with him on the more comfortable folding lawn chair and me on the makeshift wooden bench. I figured it was a fair trade; I got the cot, he got the better chair. Although I had asked Master Akio many times if he wanted the cot, he always said he was perfectly happy and content sleeping on the ground. But he did say sleeping with a blanket was a real treat.

I turned to Master Akio after my first mouthful of food, "The food tastes wonderful. You did a great job at spicing everything. Very tasty."

He turned and faced me. "You are welcome."

We both sat in silence, listening to the peaceful ocean waves lap onto the sandy shore as we once again immersed ourselves in the sunset. I think this was my twelfth spectacular sunset in a row and I had yet to tire of them. The colors seemed more vibrant here than anywhere else I've ever been. The sun was continually framed within deep shades of orange. And I always felt like the last rays of sun were reaching out to me to offer their last bit of heat.

Normally, we would've had a fire lit by now, but I was far too tired to stay awake much longer. Quietly, I stood up, gathered my plate and coffee cup, and began preparations for our nightly cleanup. While I waited for the water to boil, I poured myself a cup of coffee and brought the teapot to the living room for Master Akio so that he could have another cup of tea before bed. In a silent gesture of appreciation, he simply nodded his head as I poured tea into his cup. Quietly, I sat back down on my bench facing the ocean, to enjoy the last few moments of the now fading sunset.

It did not take us long to clean up the kitchen, wash and dry the dishes, and put everything away into its proper place. With everything packed away for the night, I turned to Master Akio and said, "I'm very tired. I worked really hard today. I am going to bed. Good night."

"I go to bed in a moment. Good night, Graham."

Day Thirteen

I heard Master Akio's covers gently rustle next to me. If it wasn't already getting light in the tent I would've sworn he was just coming to bed and not that it was time to get up. I rolled over with a groan, "Is it time to get up already? I didn't even hear you come to bed last night."

Master Akio smiled and teased me, "You snore when you very tired and you very, very, *very* tired last night. You snore very long and very loud. How you hear Akio come in?"

With a slightly sheepish grin I protested, "Me, snore?"

Master Akio finished rolling up his blanket and said, "Shelling of Wotje Atoll during war not so loud as you snore last night!"

"I am sorry." Was all I could think to say; I was embarrassed to have disturbed his sleep.

He chuckled, "No need say sorry. You work hard yesterday. You snore make Akio think many times I not sleep during war because so many men snore. Many times alone on this island I ask to see friends and hear snore again." He chuckled again. "I not see friends, but Universe give me Graham and loud snore!"

"So, Master Akio, what you are saying is that I should be careful what I wish for?"

He paused as a serious look washed over his face, "Yes, you ask for what you *really* want, then let go, and not expect.

Akio want see friends. Snore is way to remember friends. Universe not possible give back friends, so give way to remember friends."

Master Akio's words struck a chord deep inside of me. It was like I knew what he was saying, but at the same time, I had no idea what he had just said. As I finished tidying up the tent, I kept turning his words over and over in my mind.

My thinking was interrupted by the increasing temperatures inside the tent. It had begun to feel like a super-heated sauna, signaling time to get out and start the day. As part of our morning ritual we each took a bottle of water to the living room to begin our day in meditation. After a quick sip of water I settled down to begin. I focused and concentrated only on my breathing. I concentrated on the inhalation, feeling my belly slowly rise. I concentrated on the exhalation and felt my belly fall. I felt my belly rise and fall a second time and then lost focus and had to start all over again.

I must have let out a sigh or a grunt or something, letting Master Akio know that I was struggling with my meditation. He quietly asked, "What wrong? What you thinking, Graham?"

"I don't know how to explain it. Today, it is like my mind and body are at war. As I try to think about and grasp this concept of asking the Universe for help and the Universe providing help, my body says yes. But my mind says no, and the effects are a headache and an upset stomach."

"When mind and body at war, this best time to meditate. Time to ask big questions. You ask if big energy outside you have purpose. Different way to ask - is there God?"

I opened my eyes and turned towards Master Akio, "I think that's the part that's got me in turmoil. I don't know if I believe in God. I know when we were sparring I could feel this unconscious knowing guiding my body. But I don't know if I'm ready to accept that that could be God, or the Universe as you call it."

He smiled a deep, understanding smile, "Graham, this something good to meditate on! Close eyes and go back to meditation. See what comes." Reluctantly, I turned to face the ocean. I got comfortable once again on my make-shift bench and stared out at the ocean for a few long minutes, calming my mind. Gradually, I closed my eyes to slowly begin my meditation.

I heard Master Akio stir in the chair next to me and I guessed our meditation for the morning was over. Gradually, I let go of my focus on my breath and allowed my focus to return to the beach and our island. I was slightly disappointed that no big revelation had come to me, but I truly wasn't surprised. It seemed that the first lesson I had to learn was always going to be patience. When I found that, the other lessons just seemed to show up. With a slow, extended stretch, I got up off of the bench, mentally preparing for the usual morning exercises.

Master Akio led me through a series of stretches before I started my run down the beach towards the Dog Leg. It wasn't until I was about 50 yards away from camp and on my return trip that I realized I ran the whole thing. I had never run this far! This was going to be a great day. I ran all the way into camp excitedly yelling at the top of my lungs, "Master Akio! Master Akio! I ran all the way there and back without stopping! Isn't that great?"

Master Akio smiled and did his little happy dance as a way of showing that he was happy for me. "Great! What you want for breakfast for celebration of great feat?" he yelled back.

"I would like fried potatoes and eggs, some toast, and a cup of coffee. I'll be right back to help you with breakfast. I just need to walk a little." Without waiting for a response, I began walking back towards the Dog Leg to stretch my legs and catch my breath.

By the time I returned to camp, Master Akio had the potatoes peeled and the coffee and tea already on the stove. Since I wasn't the one cooking this morning, I decided to get the dishes ready. I poured myself a fresh cup of coffee and a cup of tea for Master Akio while he finished cooking breakfast. I was genuinely surprised when I saw the plateful Master Akio dished out for me. He saw my surprised expression and replied, "Graham, you have big days ahead. You need energy."

"Thank You!"

After a leisurely breakfast, we cleaned as usual. We even found a little extra time to do some laundry, washing t-shirts and shorts. Once the cleaning was done, it was time to go work on our temple. We collected all the necessary tools and half a dozen bottles of water.

We placed our offerings inside the temple area and then spent the better part of the morning building a small stool and bench for Master Akio to sit on while he weaved the grass mats. We worked together in relative silence, although now and then I had to request help or get further instructions. While I was capable of doing a lot of things, this woodcraft stuff was way, way beyond my skill level.

When the bench and stool were finished, we walked back to camp in silence for a quick lunch of biscuits and soup. As we were eating, I suddenly stopped, put my spoon down, and looked at Master Akio. "What do you think our temple will look like? I really have no idea what it will look like because we haven't even talked about it yet. You just said we were building a temple and I blindly followed along."

"Good question. I wonder when you ask me what we build. Old Temple take many months to build. Need different way to build Summer Temple. We use mats for walls and floors. Palm leaves for roof." He looked at me and smiled. "When you come back for longer time, we build stronger temple."

My stomach began churning. I slowly came to the realization that I did not like the thought of leaving this island. I knew that Master Akio and I were going to have discuss my departure, and soon. My stomach got worse at the thought of leaving the island - and Master Akio – but I said nothing.

Once we cleaned up our lunch dishes, we walked back to the temple construction site where we spent most of the remainder of the afternoon working separately. I spent the afternoon blessing, then chopping down countless trees and dragging them back to our construction site. It was tough and tiring work. Master Akio spent the afternoon weaving square grass mats. I really don't know who got the worst job. I wasn't sure I could really spend the day sitting in one spot, weaving grass mats.

After what seemed like countless hours of mindless chopping and dragging the various trees needed for the Summer Temple, Master Akio finally signaled to me. It was time to go fishing. We cleaned up our construction site and took our tools and offerings back to the summer camp.

As we were putting the tools away in their respective places Master Akio surprised me by saying, "Graham, before we go fishing, put kettle on for tea, please."

"I thought you wanted to go fishing?"

He replied with a calm, gentle, but very firm tone, "Yes." I knew I was just to make the tea and ask no further questions at this point in time.

As I bustled about making tea, I wondered what was up. Master Akio was a stickler for routines. Breaking our usual one meant something big was coming.

It didn't take long before the water was boiling. The tea made, we both sat in our respective chairs in our expansive beach living area. I had scrounged around in our food supplies and brought out a small package of cookies for us to share. With a nod of his head and a smile, Master Akio thanked me for the cup of tea and cookies.

We sipped our tea in an unusual, awkward silence. I was waiting for Master Akio to speak and was starting to wonder if I should say something. After about ten minutes of silence, Master Akio turned to face me. "Graham, lunch time something changed in you. I feel sadness from you. "Graham, why you sad?" I could feel Master Akio's concern for my well-being envelope my whole body. It was like someone was wrapping me up in a warm, fuzzy blanket of love. It felt pretty weird, but that was only because this was another entirely new experience for me. Genuine concern was not something I experienced often.

I turned my head and then my whole body so I could face him directly. "Master Akio, I was sad at lunchtime and I am still sad because I suddenly realized I am leaving the island in seventeen days and I don't know if you are coming with me or if I am leaving you here."

Master Akio's face broke into a huge smile, "Graham, good question. I know, I not know now." He took a sip of his tea and his face took on a somber expression, "I also sad because I not know many things. I not know if my family alive. My friends all die in shelling on Wojte Atoll. Japan now not Japan I remember. Graham, I not leave this island for many years, but I feel energy of earth change. I know world I leave long time ago not same world you go home to. So, Graham don't be sad, we talk more about this later."

We sipped our tea in silence for a few more moments, lost in our own thoughts. Master Akio eventually broke our silence. "We finish tea and go fishing!"

"That sounds good." After taking the last sip from my cup and a glance out over the bay, I carried our cups back to the kitchen.

The sun had been down for a long time already, but neither of us was ready for bed. We were enjoying sitting around the campfire and lavishly embellishing the stories of our day's fishing exploits. We'd both managed to spear a couple of rather large fish. This took quite a bit of skill, so we were rather proud of our accomplishments. Now we were having fun re-telling the tales and playfully bragging. It had been a couple days since we just sat around the campfire and talked. It was a great evening.

Days Fourteen to Seventeen

The next four days seemed to blur together. I was either chopping trees, dragging trees, or weaving mats with Master Akio. He could weave three mats to my one. The weaving was very hard on my fingers, so it made journaling a very sore and difficult process. Master Akio would hear none of my complaining and, despite my boisterous protests on how much my fingers hurt or how much he needed my help, he made sure I spent time journaling each afternoon.

It was my seventeenth day on the island when Master Akio, walking around the pile of mats, said with a pleased look on his face, "Tomorrow we build Summer Temple."

Thank goodness! I don't know how many more mats my fingers can take. But I didn't want to admit it out loud.

Master Akio smiled his impish grin that always told me he was about to say something witty. "Graham, you cannot quit now! Your mats just start to be good. Hmmm. You weave again first mats you make."

I looked up with mock horror on my face, screaming, "Noooooooo!"

"Redo mats or let me catch biggest fish today! What your choice, Graham?"

I bent down and picked up another palm frond. "I think I'll weave some more mats!" I laughed.

"What? You not let old man fish better? You have no compassion for old people?"

"I don't see an old man in front of me. I see a Master who has taught his student too well and now doesn't want to lose to that student.

Master Akio smiled, "Who says I lose to you? Today contest. You choose - biggest fish or most fish?"

I stood to gather the tools and replied, "The biggest."

Master Akio grinned from ear to ear like a kid going to the candy store. "Loser cook and clean after supper," he said.

I swung the backpack full of tools over my shoulder and started towards camp. "Deal."

As I brought Master Akio his supper, I couldn't help but smile to myself. I should've known better than to trust that crafty, old man I affectionately call Master. He got the biggest fish all right. He got the biggest fish that we'd ever caught. It was huge! We wouldn't have to go fishing for at least two more days… that's as long as I figured the cooked fish would keep without any dry ice left in the coolers.

When he finished his meal, Master Akio said, with that impish grin on his face, "You see how big fish I caught?"

"Yes, I saw how big it was," I replied as I gathered our dishes. While I did the washing by myself, Master Akio took childish and great delight in repeatedly asking me who caught the biggest fish. I played along with him by always answering, "I don't know who caught the biggest fish. Why don't you tell

140

me, Master Akio?" This provided him the opportunity to further embellish the size of his fish and enhance the drama surrounding the experience of spearing it. Before long we were both howling in fits of laughter with the ever-changing and evolving story of the bet and the actual catching of the fish.

Day Eighteen

I heard Master Akio stir in the tent beside me. Peering through my barely opened eyes I mustered, "Is it time to get up already?" Through my sleep filled eyes I could see Master Akio smiling. "Yes, we go meditate."

Groggily I got up, made my bed and tidied up the tent before meeting Master Akio on the beach to do our morning meditation. My entire body felt like lead. It felt like someone had driven over me in the middle of the night. I was truly not used to working this physically hard and my body was reminding me with numerous aches and pains.

I hobbled over to Master Akio and sat down on my bench. He smiled at me and placed his right hand on my shoulder. "You work hard for many days. Today we do stretching and meditate before breakfast. I cook special breakfast. You walk to corner of island and back. No running today."

I was relieved to hear that I didn't have to run today. I smiled at him with sincere gratitude.

Today's stretching routine was very gentle and mild. I really enjoyed it and my body felt so much better afterwards. When we finished, we both returned to our seats. Once we'd settled in, Master Akio turned to me. I could feel his soft, gentle energy. "Graham, today is about love. This sacred and special day because we put love in everything we do.

142

Everything we do now - today and after today - is about love. You understand?"

Before I could reply, Master Akio continued, "Graham, you remember we talk about how everything is sacred?" He didn't wait for my reply, "Everything is sacred. Everything is energy. Thinking is energy. This bench you sit on is energy. Everything around us, and in us, is energy. When we build something with love energy, it has love energy. When we build something with angry energy, it has angry energy. Today we build with love energy. We build Summer Temple with love, so it have love energy."

Master Akio paused. I could sense he was searching for words, trying to figure out how to say what he was feeling. I remained quiet, which was a miracle in itself, because the old Graham wasn't too good at giving anyone the opportunity to collect their thoughts.

Eventually Master Akio asked, "Graham, you walk into room with people and know something not right? Many years ago when I young boy in Japan, I walk into my house and I know something not right. I very young and not know what not right, but now I know I feel energy of Mother and Father fight."

He paused again. With an inquisitive look on his face he asked, "Graham, you walk in very old temple?"

I knew Master Akio wanted me to answer this question. "I have not been in a temple, but I have been inside some very old churches, which would be like a temple."

Master Akio excitedly nodded his head and said, "Good! You feel different energy inside from outside of temple?"

I nodded my head in agreement, "Yes, the old churches were very sacred and just being in them calmed me down. I don't know if I can put words to it, but the energy was different."

Master Akio responded, "Inside temple, you feel energy of builders and intentions of all people who visit temple. When we build our temple - and every time we go inside temple - we create energy. Today you meditate on energy you want in our temple."

I turned away from Master Akio and looked out over the ocean for few moments. Looking out at the ocean, or even picturing it in my mind, always made me feel very calm. I was always able to center and let go of the clutter in my thoughts when I began my meditation with a view of the ocean.

I don't know how long I'd been lost in my morning meditation but it seemed longer than normal. The morning sun had already moved quite a bit, confirming that this meditation had been deeper and longer than usual. Master Akio got up and went to the kitchen, directing me to walk to the Dog Leg and back. "No running today," he reminded me.

I walked over to the coolers, pulled out a bottle of water and began my walk. I was feeling very peaceful, excited and full of wonder; not just because we were building a temple, but because we were doing something I'd never done before. I had no idea what it would look like and what I was supposed to do to help build it. In short, I had no idea what was going on. I didn't have a plan. Or rather, I didn't know the plan. I was not in charge and I didn't know what was expected of me. In a crazy, exciting way, it seemed perfect for the new Graham Alexander Connelly. The old Graham would've been on the verge of a nervous breakdown or a panic attack, but the new Graham was really okay with this approach.

As I walked back into camp I cheerfully asked, "What's for breakfast?"

Master Akio looked up from his cooking with a smile, "Good timing!"

I was a little surprised to see that we were having rice, water, and tea for breakfast. Master Akio explained, "To honour simplicity of our temple, we eat simple today."

After eating our humble, yet wholesome breakfast, we cleaned up the kitchen area and were soon on our way to begin assembling our temple. I was pumped to finally put it together after five physically demanding days of chopping, hauling, and weaving. It would be good to build it and finally be able to use it.

I must have snorted or chuckled then because Master Akio looked over to me and asked what I was thinking about. I chuckled and said, "Master Akio, I have been focused on building a temple and now I'm really excited about building the Summer Temple. But I don't even know why. I have never been in a temple, besides yours, so I don't know what we are going to do inside it. Well, maybe meditate, but that's all I can really think of. What will we do in there? Why are we building a temple?"

A slow, sly smile crept across Master Akio's face. He lifted his arm and promptly cuffed me on the back of the head. I looked at him with surprise and shock. "What was that for?"

Master Akio impishly asked, "Why you ask question now and not before?" and picked up his pace. I quickly scampered after him, the tools noisily rattling together in the backpack on my shoulders. When I caught up and fell in step with him, I said, "I didn't ask questions because I thought I was the student and you would teach me when it was the right time."

Master Akio continued walking towards the temple and I could sense he was trying to sort out what to say. Finally, he stopped and turned to me. "Graham, you good student. You teach Master much. Thank You! I explain more." With more grace and elegance than I had ever before witnessed, he bowed to me, a slow, long, lingering, respectful bow.

I was unable to say anything to him because of the huge lump in my throat that immediately appeared from his heartfelt show of respect. I just stood there with a silly grin on my face. Master Akio smiled, turned, and continued walking up the beach. I fell back in step with him.

"Graham, master tell student many things. Some things learn, some not. When student ask question because student curious and want to learn, master answer and student learn much more. Best learning from experience, from doing things. I tell you about sword fighting or I show you sword fighting? You learn more when I show you. You learn more when you sword fight. You learn more when you ask questions after sword fight. Graham, to learn much you have to experience much and ask many questions. Please ask questions. Remember, I may not answer all questions, but always ask."

We continued on up the beach, stopping before the temple area. I spoke quietly to Master Akio, "I will ask more questions."

I discovered by merely asking a few questions, that Master Akio had me chop down so many trees so we could build a series of scaffolds and ladders to work from. These would allow us to safely lash the beams to the trees and easily place the temple's rafters in the right locations. I also learnt that we were building a temple for a whole bunch of reasons: to keep my body active – building up my fitness levels; to keep my mind active by learning new things; and to create something together that was truly ours. Master Akio also said that, "When you build own temple it become more sacred to the builders."

After a very quick lunch-break of rice, tea, and some fish soup, we spent the entire afternoon creating and placing all the rafters. As we stood on the scaffolding, pleased that the last rafter was in place, Master Akio said, "Good work. We go fishing!"

"Did you forget that you caught that huge fish yesterday and we don't need any today? We still have lots left over."

Master Akio chuckled, "I forget. We have more water here?" I scrambled down the scaffolding and checked my backpack. I yelled back up at him, "We have two full bottles and we each have a partial one."

Master Akio grinned, "Good for short walk, not long walk. Leave tools here. We go for short walk on beach. We not walk very far on this beach before."

Happy to go exploring, I agreed.

Apparently, Master Akio didn't know that 90 year old men weren't supposed to be climbing up and down scaffolding, let alone artfully and nimbly. He was standing beside me on solid ground before I knew it. We gathered up and stowed the tools in the backpack, brushed all the sawdust and tree bark off of each other's backs, and then started our walk.

We had walked for no more than five minutes when we both stopped dead in our tracks. Just in front of us was a small stream running out from the jungle; the faint but pungent odor of sulfur caught our attention. We could see small wisps of steam rising from the water. I could tell Master Akio was as excited as I was at the possibility of having our very own hot spring.

He walked quickly to the stream and lowered his hand to it, stopping just above the water to test how much heat there was. I walked into the jungle and came back with a small stick. I placed it in the water to test for acid or something equally as dangerous. I left the stick in the water for a fairly long time. When I pulled it out, we both examined it; there was no apparent damage. Master Akio seemed satisfied that the water posed no danger, so he bent down and plunged his hand into the stream. He looked at me with an excited grin, "Water not too hot. We follow stream."

The stream was fairly easy to follow since the sulfur had pretty much killed all the vegetation within five feet of the stream, and it followed a very gentle slope. We walked about 200 yards into the jungle before coming to an abrupt stop. The stream seemed to erupt from a small rock patch in front of us. Master Akio once again bent down and let his hand hover over top of the gurgling water. This time he didn't put his hand in. He looked up at me and said, "Water more hot here!"

He stood up and excitedly said, "When you come back, Graham, you bring sheet like one over kitchen table and we build hot pool. Earth too sandy here to make deep pool. Need sheet to keep water in pool." He kicked at the earth and dug in it with his hands multiple times to assess the soil conditions. Satisfied that his initial assessment was correct, he said, "Graham, when you come back, you bring sheet two times bigger than kitchen."

I was going to correct Master Akio and tell him it was a tarp, not a sheet that I was using as an awning, but then I thought, *Does it really matter? I know what he means.* I smiled realizing again how I'd changed; it would have mattered to the old Graham. It would have mattered a lot to tell Master Akio the difference just so that I could show him I was smarter and he was wrong. The old Graham couldn't be wrong, ever! Even if it meant crashing my plane to make my point, I was never wrong.

Instead, I clarified, "You only want one twice as big?"

"Yes, only twice as big."

As we stepped back onto the white sandy beach and began the short walk to the temple, Master Akio abruptly stopped and touched my arm. He looked at me with a somber expression. "Bring more beer, also. Not many. One or two beer every five or six days." He let go of my arm, smiled and continued walking towards the temple.

Supper was, purely and simply put, a feast. We had pan-fried fish steaks, rice, and canned peas topped off with chocolate pudding for dessert. We had an exquisite, completely over the top finish with a chai latte made from sweetened condensed milk. Master Akio may have eyed me suspiciously when I handed him his chai latte but after his first little tentative sip, he was hooked. "How come you not make this before? You make more?"

"We probably have enough ingredients to make you about four cups of chai latte a day, every day until I leave."

His only response was a huge grin.

After finishing his drink, Master Akio said, "I am very tired. I need go to bed." With that he bid me a good night and went off to the tent. It was unusual for Master Akio to go to bed before me. I guessed it was all the climbing up and down the various scaffolds and the other physical labor of the last few days that really tired him out.

I quickly had all our dishes washed, dried, and put away. I was probably only ten short minutes behind Master Akio as I carefully unzipped the tent and stepped inside. I could already hear him snoring ever so softly. He stirred briefly as I turned around and zipped up the tent. I think I was asleep within seconds of my head coming to rest on my pillow.

Days Nineteen and Twenty

The oppressive heat in the tent woke me with a start. I could already feel sweat pool in the small recesses of my body. We had slept later than normal. I rolled over, flipped the covers off and slowly began to stand up. I looked over just in time to see Master Akio's eyes flash open. To my astonishment, he appeared to be completely and fully awake. I hate morning people, I thought as I looked at him. Instead, I just said, "Morning, Master Akio."

Master Akio responded with a smile and an enthusiastic, "Good morning, Graham. We go meditate."

We made our beds, quickly tidied the tent, and then quietly exited to go do our morning meditation. My dislike of early mornings always evaporated within minutes of sitting down to take in the morning sunrise. I loved how the sun peeked over the trees behind camp and slowly illuminated the ocean.

After our morning meditation, a vigorous set of exercises, and a simple breakfast, we quickly cleaned up. Soon we were heading back up the beach to resume our work on the temple.

We spent the better part of the morning working on thatching the roof with palm fronds. I was surprised; thatching a roof was far easier than I thought it would be. I'd thought it would take us days to complete the roof.

Master Akio climbed down off the scaffolding and walked over to the backpack to take out two bottles of water. I heard, "Graham!" and turned my head just in time to see a bottle hurtling towards me. I calmly put down the frond I was trying to place on the roof and reached out to grab the projectile. It hit my hand with a resounding smack. I nodded my head in appreciation towards Master Akio and thanked him. I twisted the cap off the bottle, took two huge gulps of water and then turned my focus to Master Akio.

"I thought we were supposed to do everything with love. How come you threw the water bottle at me?"

Master Akio smiled, "Good question! Graham, did you see or feel me throw the water at you with anger?"

I had to admit he sort of just threw the water at me. "No, I did not feel you were angry."

"When you catch water, you feel anger? Anger because you must catch water? Anger because I throw water hard at you?"

Once again I had to admit that I did not feel any anger at Master Akio for throwing the water bottle at me or towards me and I was okay with how hard he threw it.

I quickly slid down the scaffolding and stood before him. "So, what's the lesson here?"

Master Akio smiled, "Graham, I say your word. No DRAMA. I throw water bottle to you very hard, but I throw bottle to you with no drama. You look and see water bottle come very hard and fast, but you just catch it. No drama. No story. Just fact. I throw, you catch. You ask question with no feeling. No story. You ask how come with no drama."

I smiled and looked Master Akio directly in the eyes. "So, my lesson was about drama. If I quit making up stories about why something happened, I remove the drama from my life and make my life easier?"

Master Akio squealed in delight, "Yes!"

I gave him a heartfelt bow of appreciation then turned to climb back up the scaffolding. I was just about to ascend when I spied a stick the perfect size for a make-shift sword.

As fast as possible, I reached over, grabbed the stick, and turned, ready to charge Master Akio. He wasn't there! I froze for a split second. He was just there! I frantically looked around for him. It was like he knew what I was thinking because he had leapt over to the middle of the temple and was grabbing his sword - the sword he had made as his offering - the sword that was balanced and had a hilt to protect his hand. I realized I had lost any advantage that surprise had given me. Master Akio had the advantage of higher ground and a better weapon.

I read *The Art of War* by Sun Tze many years ago and I was struck with the sudden realization that the book was right. I knew this battle was already over. Even before the first blow was struck, I had already lost. So, I did the only thing a good student of war who had just challenged his master would do, I went to one knee. I held out my weapon horizontally above my head with both hands, bowed my head, and solemnly spoke, "I surrender."

I heard Master Akio walk towards me. I kept my head down. I saw his feet stop in front of me. I felt him take my makeshift sword from my outstretched hands. He quietly spoke, "I accept."

I felt Master Akio grasp my hand in an offer to help me up from the ground. I slowly stood up and lifted my eyes to look at him. He looked puzzled. "Why you surrender?"

"As soon as I saw you with your sword and I only had a stick as a weapon, I knew it was over for me. So, I made the choice to live to fight another day. I felt I didn't know how, or have enough experience, to beat you. I knew I needed to learn more."

Master Akio smiled, "There is truth in your words and your actions, Graham. Someday in future I teach you no more; you know everything I know. We spar and you beat me. Then you are ready to be Master. Now you are still Student. It is good you understand lessons from this." He paused. "I miss our sword fight. Tomorrow morning we spar again."

I recalled our last fight and felt concern for Master Akio's health. My face must have betrayed my thoughts, for he smiled at me and spoke, "Graham, our sword fights have much drama. You want to prove much to yourself. You have much pride in sparring. Tomorrow, we spar with no drama. No pride.

155

We spar to learn Kendo – The Way of Sword. Graham, I am old man. When we spar with drama you can beat old man. But when you learn from a place of love and no drama, I still teach you much."

For the second time this day, I bowed to Master Akio. "I look forward to tomorrow's lessons."

With that, we both turned and climbed up the scaffolding to continue our work on the roof.

We completed thatching the roof and then broke for a simple lunch of rice, tea, and canned chicken; we had finally eaten all of the fish from our very successful fishing contest. I was looking forward to going fishing again tonight. With that thought I turned to Master Akio, "Our contest was fun, but I don't think we should catch another fish that big again."

Master Akio looked puzzled, "Why not, Graham?"

"We have lots of food so we really don't need to catch a fish every day for survival. But I really like going fishing every day. If we catch a huge fish like you did, that means we don't need to go fishing every day."

Master Akio looked up to the heavens, and with mock horror in his voice said, "Oh, great Universe. Why this student ask hard question?" With a huge grin, he turned and faced me. "Graham, that is best question you ask."

I was puzzled. "But, Master Akio, I didn't ask a question."

"No, but there is truth in your statement. Graham, I tell you something and ask you question. Then you go for walk. You walk back to Old Home and pick tomatoes and lettuce from garden. Bring back for supper." Master Akio knew I was going to object, so he quickly added, "You do this simply because I ask. You do it with no question."

Master Akio continued, suddenly sounding like a storyteller, "Graham, we meditate every morning. We stretch our bodies and exercise every morning. Every afternoon you write in your journal. Why?" It appeared to be a rhetorical question so I did not answer. He continued, "Because we learn to clear our minds and create discipline. Discipline good for all life, now and in future. We love fishing. Fishing is great training. Fishing is exercise for mind, body, and spirit. Fishing also give us food. Graham, I ask you question and then you ask no question or say no more. You get two or three water bottles, your backpack, and a small towel for tomatoes and lettuce. You walk and you think about question. See everything around you and in you. Graham, no need to hurry back. Take time with question."

Master Akio stood up and turned away from me. He walked towards the ocean, "Graham, when is discipline not discipline?"

I knew I had been dismissed to go on my quest, so I got up and walked to the coolers. I grabbed three bottles of water, emptied the tools from the backpack, and shook it out to clean the debris from the bottom of the pack. I put two small towels and the water in the pack, grabbed my camera, and left camp.

It felt kind of weird to leave in the midst of building the temple and have Master Akio send me off in the manner he did. Actually, it felt really weird, but I did agree to his training style. Though the old Graham was fuming and really indignant - *How dare that old man send me away, who the hell does he think he is?* The new Graham actually found it a bit exciting.

Here I was, Graham Alexander Connelly, starting out on my very first quest at 42 years of age. Though the budding romantic explorer in me kind of hoped it would be for something greater, like a sword or mystical scrolls, I decided that a quest is a quest. I was tasked with discovering when discipline is not discipline. *Hmmm. When is discipline not discipline? That's a great question. But auugghhhh!* What the heck is discipline in the first place? I make my bed every morning... is that discipline? Auagghhh! This was not going to be easy.

I had walked all the way to the Dog Leg before I even realized I had not paid any attention to my surroundings at all! None, zip, zero attention. The quest given to me was to observe myself and my surroundings. Well, I had succeeded in observing and being very aware of my thoughts, but I had no idea what I had walked past. I was already at the Dog Leg and I hadn't seen a darn thing. So, with a bit of muttering under my breath, I did the only thing I could think to do: I turned around and walked back to camp. This was my first quest and I was going to do this right. I had no idea what Master Akio thought as I marched back through the camp. Truthfully, I really wasn't too concerned. I was too intent on doing my quest the best I could.

Roughly ten yards or so from camp I spun around and stopped, facing the way I had just come from. I stood there for a long while, focusing on my breathing and clearing my head.

Once my thoughts had slowed to a moderate pace, I started walking slowly toward the Dog Leg again. Tentatively, I began to observe my surroundings, just noticing things close by on the beach to begin with. At first, I only saw the small pebbles on the beach, but then I was amazed to see small hermit crabs scuttling along the sand, which I had never seen before. As I grew more confident in my ability to observe, I was able to see many things at once - the butterfly at the edge of the jungle on my left hand side, the fish jumping in ocean on my right side, the numerous birds in the sky above, the shells and crabs on the beach in front of me. The old Graham began screaming inside, *You can't do this! It is impossible to see in all directions at once; you'll just give yourself a headache.* Ignoring him, I continued up the beach, repeatedly practicing and expanding my ability to see all of my surroundings at once.

As I passed my old crash campsite, I could now clearly see the damage Blaine and I had done to the jungle. I didn't notice any of this on my previous trip to the site, but now I could see we had broken off branches and uprooted small trees for our shelter and fire. There were 'holes' in the patches of grasses where we'd ripped out clumps of grass. I was appalled at the destruction we had caused. I was driven, or should I say guided, to stop before each of the trees we broke or damaged and offer a small blessing in the form of a heartfelt thank you.

The sheer notion of blessing a stupid tree had the old Graham spitting nails and his mind erupted into convulsions. He had finally had enough. He took hold of the under-developed infant mind of the new Graham and smashed it against the closest tree. He slammed it hard and screamed, *What the hell are you doing?* The sheer ferocity of the old Graham's attack was staggering and excruciatingly painful. I was overcome with a massive stomachache and a nearly debilitating headache. The effect had me doubled over in pain to the point that I thought I would throw up.

I closed my eyes and began focusing on my breathing, "Breathe out, breath in... Focus only on the breath..."

It was a frantic and desperate measure on my part. I was just trying to calm my mind so I could free myself from this crazy, instant blinding headache. It took all the effort I could muster to remain focused. I could still hear the old Graham desperately screaming, Don't you shut me out like this! I could feel my heart begin to race; I was in the midst of an intense panic attack. I had a blistering headache and the most intense stomach cramps of my life. The old Graham had successfully conjured up my greatest torture.

All of a sudden, an inexplicable soothing feeling overtook my body, calming my soul and spirit. In the midst of the pain, I felt peaceful.

It again felt like my mind was abruptly ripped out of my head and thrown into the far frozen reaches of the universe where it exploded into a gazillion little pieces. If that wasn't enough, each of those pieces further exploded into a million tiny pieces. I could feel and sense my essence just floating around in this cosmic energetic void. The void contained nothing, while at the same time containing everything and all possibilities.

It was from this void that I came face to face with the realization that I could choose what to put back into the vessel I called Graham. I had the choice of what to collect from all the exploded pieces; from all the bits of me. With this slow dawning rose a new understanding within my consciousness. I came to an absolute understanding that I, Graham Alexander Connelly, could actively and willingly choose to behave in a particular way in any given moment. I was so overwhelmed by the freedom and responsibility of this idea that I doubled over in simultaneous sobs of horror and peals of laughter.

My diaphragm aching from the uncontrollable fits of laughter, sand caked to my face where it mixed with my tears, I realized that life could be so simple if I would just take absolute control of my life and live from this choice. It was possible to live without blaming myself or others.

I completely lost all track or sense of time, though at some point during my experience I became aware of the sun. Initially, I thought the sun was setting, but after some careful observation I realized that the temperature was actually rising and not cooling off. I was so confused for a few long moments until I realized the colours changing in the sky were over the jungle, not the water. This was a sun rise. I had missed out on the sunset and it was already morning. I was stunned. This meant I was on the beach laughing and crying to myself for nearly eighteen hours! I must have passed out at some point during my ordeal. Could some of the battle with old Graham have been a dream?

With the uneasiness of a toddler taking his first, tentative steps, I stood up slowly and with caution. My legs tingled intensely as the blood began to circulate fully once again. I stood there, unable to move for a long time. When I felt ready to move again, I slowly, and to the best of my still fuzzy memory, replicated Master Akio's morning stretches. It felt weird to do them without him – but I was able to do all of the exercises and in the same order.

After completing my stretching routine, my body was able, ready, and willing to continue my journey on up the island towards Master Akio's home. As I walked along the beach, I felt fully alive for the first time. I observed small crabs scuttling around the various rocky outcroppings. I heard a sea gull for the second time since being on the island. I even noticed small and large bits of plastic that had washed up on the shore. I was astounded by this. We were hundreds of miles from other islands and yet evidence of mankind was washed up even on this isolated paradise. I saw coconuts in the surf, coconuts on the ground, coconuts everywhere - I marveled at this. Had the number of coconuts on the island multiplied overnight? I'd never noticed any here before.

This morning it felt like I was not only seeing more but that I was seeing everything for the very first time. It was as if the colours of the trees, the ocean, and the sky were all more vibrant. It was like my eyes were new and had never seen before. It was such an amazing feeling to see the world as if it was new. I had never noticed how the sand crunched slightly with each footstep. The warm water from my bottle was refreshing. It was like my whole body rejoiced in pure bliss with every swallow!

Without any difficulty, I found the tiny opening in the jungle that was the path leading to Master Akio's home. Just before leaving the beach, I stopped and looked out across the expansive crystal blue ocean. I never tired of the view, and today it seemed particularly spectacular. I spied the small chain of islands off to my left - the islands that Blaine and I swam and walked from to get to this island - their green shapes rising up out of the ocean. I decided that on one of my next trips, I would re-walk our route.

As I turned and entered the path into the jungle, I was struck with the knowledge that on my next trip back here I would bring Blaine. I had been having these strange moments of just knowing things ever since meeting Master Akio. I chuckled out loud. I didn't know how I was going to talk him into it or convince him to come. All I knew was that he needed to come here with me next time.

Before I could see Master Akio's home I could smell it. The odors of his homestead were distinct. I breathed in deeply, taking in the various pleasing fragrances of the flowers and the vegetable garden. I was surprised that I could also taste and smell the fresh water in the air instead of the salt from the sea. I paused and for the first time allowed myself to really hear the jungle noises. There were crickets singing. I looked around and saw the jungle teaming with life; spiders, centipedes and various beetles were all hard at work.

I sensed I was near my destination. Master Akio's home was like a gigantic, energetic oasis of peace and calm in the midst of a whirlwind of chaos. The island was teaming with chaos - birth and death – the jungle was in a continuous state of new beginnings: ocean waves crashing in on the island, leaves falling from the tree top canopy, birds eating insects, insects being born.

I walked past Master Akio's home and continued on down towards the garden, stopping briefly to check out its state. All looked well so I went straight to the pond. I dropped my backpack and then stripped off my clothes and eagerly jumped into the deep fresh water. The cool water was delightful and I swam and frolicked for quite some time. Gradually, I made my way up to the stream that filled the pool, drinking deeply from the cool fresh water. I swam back towards my backpack and carefully exited the pond. I stood in the warm morning sun to dry myself before I put my clothes back on. I retrieved the water bottles from the backpack and refilled them with fresh stream water.

With my thirst sated and my water bottles filled, I meandered back to Master Akio's temple. I slipped off my shoes, then opened the small gate and entered the temple area. I walked into the temple proper and sat down. It felt very peaceful and calm sitting here, although it did feel a bit funny without Master Akio.

As I sat, I began to look around the temple walls, carefully examining the construction. I was trying to figure out how he built it. I didn't see any lashing in the temple at all. It looked like Master Akio had built this temple using various friction-fit joints or something like that. I figured that would be a lot more work, and a lot more time consuming than just lashing poles together. I wondered how long it took him to build.

I sat in the temple for a long time meditating and contemplating life and the question of my quest: when is discipline no longer discipline? I meditated, I sat, and I contemplated. I turned the question over and over in my mind and nothing came to me. Suddenly, a strange feeling - or inexplicable calling - urged me to go pick the tomatoes and lettuce right away and make my way back to my camp.

I closed the gate behind me and made the short trek to the garden. I spent about ten minutes carefully selecting just the right tomatoes, checking each one for ripeness and firmness. Once I had selected about half a dozen bright red tomatoes, I carefully wrapped them with the two towels I brought. I then moved over to the lettuce. Lettuce was much easier and far faster to pick - I just used my pocket knife to cut the plants. I was about to leave when I spied the carrots. I carefully plucked out fifteen large, vibrant orange ones; some for a snack on the trip home and the rest to go with supper tonight. And as I pulled them up I actually smelled the musty aroma of the dirt for the first time in my life. I had to smile as I thought it smelled 'earthy'.

With carrots in hand, I walked back to the cool, fresh water pool and quickly washed them. I packed them in the backpack, careful not to squish the ripe tomatoes, and started the long walk home.

As I rounded the Dog Leg, I could vaguely make out the camp in the distance. As I got closer to our Summer Home,

I could see that Master Akio was in the kitchen doing something. I picked up my pace and in no time at all, I was walking back into camp.

"Welcome home, Graham." Master Akio handed me a cup of fresh coffee. "You want to talk now and go fishing after? Or go fishing now and talk after supper?"

I smiled and took the coffee. "Thank you for the coffee. I think I would like to go fishing with you, make supper, and then sit around the campfire and talk."

"Good idea. Good thing I get more wood, huh?"

I glanced over to the wood pile. It was huge! I knew what Master Akio had done for most of his day; we had lots of fire wood now.

I leisurely finished my cup of delicious hot coffee, savoring every rich flavorful mouthful while master Akio sat in his chair drinking his tea. After we both finished our drinks, I got up from my bench and put the cups in the dishwashing pan. I collected the spear gun and snorkel from the containers and we waded into the ocean. We alternated between fishing and playing in the waves for the better part of an hour.

I decided to take one last turn at fishing for the day.

I was swimming along underwater, checking out a small rock on the ocean floor when I sensed a huge fish swimming towards me. I could not see him coming - he was approaching me from behind – but somehow I knew he was there and would be within easy spear range as he passed me.

My heart beat faster from the sheer excitement that I was going to spear a big fish and claim bragging rights. Also, just knowing he was out there even without seeing him was truly exhilarating.

Slowly, I turned towards the fish. I raised the spear gun and carefully aimed, my finger resting on the trigger. The huge fish continued to swim towards me. This would be the biggest fish I'd ever caught, even bigger than Master Akio's. I could feel my heart pounding in my chest and ears. This was so exciting! I could hardly believe my luck. It seemed like I could almost reach out and touch the massive fish. I couldn't miss with my spear gun; it was already locked and loaded.

Little by little I lowered the spear gun. *We don't need to catch another fish for supper. We already have plenty and I don't need to spear the fish just to claim bragging rights.* We had already caught a couple smaller fish for supper. As best as I could with a snorkel in my mouth, I smiled and waved the fish on with a quick blessing. I watched him swim away.

I was startled to find Master Akio watching me. I hadn't noticed him swim up. Master Akio motioned me to swim to the surface, so I did. We surfaced near each other. Master Akio looked at me, "Why you no spear fish?" As best as one can do while treading water, I shrugged my shoulders and said, "We didn't need the food and it seemed wrong to kill it just so I could say I got the biggest fish." Master Akio smiled and nodded his head, letting me know he understood. Without speaking, we both knew it was time to head in. We leisurely swam back to shore. It was supper time.

Supper once again was a feast fit for kings: flat bread, pasta, fish, canned green beans, the fresh tomatoes, lettuce, and a few of the crisp carrots from the garden. I didn't know whether I was exceptional hungry or whether my experience on the beach affected my taste buds, but the food tasted like it was prepared by a gourmet chef. Had I been alone, I would have even licked the plate clean.

After everything was cleaned up for the night, we both sat in our living room and enjoyed the sunset. With my new eyes, the colors seemed even more vibrant and I was stunned into silence by their sheer beauty.

Master Akio got up from his chair, "I make more tea, you like more coffee?"

"Yes that would be great. I guess I'll get the fire going then." Master Akio nodded and went off to prepare our hot drinks.

I walked up to the fire pit and placed my hands carefully over top of it to see if there was enough heat to light a fire without matches. There wasn't, so off I went to the containers for the matches and lighter fluid. With the kindling carefully prepared by Master Akio, I carefully arranged the wood as Blaine had taught me to. He said there was an art to fire building and I had come to agree with him. I added my personal touch, the lighter fluid, and struck the match. In no time at all I had successfully lit another fire. "Thank you Blaine," I whispered in the wind. I wondered if he would somehow know he was appreciated.

I put away the matches and lighter fluid and returned to my bench to enjoy the fire. It didn't take long before Master Akio arrived carrying our hot drinks.

Long after the sun had set, we sat staring into the fire, both of us lost in our own thoughts. Master Akio finally broke the silence. "Graham, when is discipline not discipline?"

I looked up and at Master Akio, then smiled and softly spoke, "When the discipline does not serve your higher good and does not put you in touch with God, or, as you prefer to say, the Universe."

Master Akio nodded his head, letting me know he was listening. *That's something I need to do when I go back home. I am a terrible listener.* I smiled at my realization and continued on with my explanation, "Let me give you an example, Master Akio. Our daily fishing is good for me and it helps me with a lot of skills that I could and do use, but it doesn't directly serve my divine or my higher purpose. So, in my case, fishing is not discipline. Now, let's say I lived on an island in a village and it was my job to be the fisherman. The daily ritual of practicing and honing my skills would be discipline, because it ultimately serves my higher self. My higher self wants me to be of service to others."

Master Akio was listening intently so I continued. "Many things or activities can teach me discipline."

Master Akio slowly raised his hand to interrupt me. "You very close to what I know, Graham. We talk more about when discipline is not discipline when you come back to island."

Master Akio must have seen my hurt expression, as I really thought I had answered the question correctly and was disappointed in his response. "Graham, you not wrong, but with more training, your answer be more deep."

I stared into the fire and thought about what Master Akio was trying to tell me for a few moments before I answered. "I think I understand what you are saying. Flying a plane is flying a plane, but as I flew different planes and logged more hours, my understanding and skill at flying broadened and deepened."

I looked up at Master Akio. He was staring at me intently. I smiled, doing my best at imitating his impish grin, "So, what you're saying is that my mind isn't developed enough to give a broad enough answer?"

Master Akio grinned, "Graham, your mind is developed much. Now you have stiff thinking. You need see all things with child's mind - see things as first time."

I just about fell off the bench when Master Akio mentioned seeing things for the first time. I promptly launched into the story of my crazy, life-changing experience on the beach the night before. How colours looked brighter, sounds were crisper and food even tasted better. I felt completely reborn. Master Akio asked many questions. I was not to leave out any detail regarding my experience, no matter how insignificant I may have felt it to be.

It was very late before we each climbed into our bed. In only seconds we were asleep.

Day Twenty-One

I heard Master Akio stirring next to me. I could feel the familiar heat begin to build within the confines of our tent. It was time to get up, time to start the day, time to work on our temple. We both quietly exited the tent, heading over to our seats on the beach. Within moments we had eased into our meditation.

Slowly, I became aware of the sound of the waves and the tropical heat on my body. I opened my eyes to find Master Akio's nose touching mine. We were face to face. I could clearly see the mischievous sparkle in his shiny black eyes. Though his presence startled me and I wanted to jump back – I had never been so close to a man - I fought to stay calm and controlled. I responded with a long, drawn out, "Yeeeeesssss?"

Master Akio smiled as he stood, "You go deep in meditation today. Very good. Now you lead stretches."

I smiled and said in my best whiny, childish voice, "But Master Akio, why do I have to lead? How come I always get the hard jobs?"

Master Akio almost choked at my unexpected burst of child-like humour and roared with laughter. Finally he managed, in his most parent-like voice, "Because I say so."

We laughed our way through the stretches.

After a simple breakfast of oatmeal and tinned fruit we quickly cleaned up, grabbed some water, and our tools. Soon, we were on our way to the temple. I was excited and looking forward the day's construction.

We stopped on the beach, just in front of the temple area. Master Akio surveyed the temple construction site. "We finish today if no problem. If problem, we finish early tomorrow."

"Really?" I was shocked.

Master Akio nodded. I was overwhelmed at how fast the walls, or rather half walls, were going up. We attached half walls to the lower half of the temple. These were part of the actual structure. The upper half of each wall was removable, or rather, moveable. They would be attached to the lower walls with grass ropes that worked like giant hinges. Each upper panel was then tied to the rafters so they would stay up when needed. If we wanted light in the temple we would simply untie the rope at the top. Once I understood what Master Akio was doing, all I could say was, "This hinged half wall is a great idea."

Master Akio smiled, "I learn this from experience. I build first temple very good. No water get in. But big problem - no light get in. Always dark, very dark place. I tear down first temple and build again".

I chuckled, "So, our temple is getting the benefit of your experience."

"Yes!"

We only took a quick break for lunch and then we were back at the temple site, hard at work. We both knew we could get the temple completed today and we were working hard to ensure that it happened. The hardest job was putting in the floor. Master Akio had me cut what seemed like hundreds of small, long trees that were all approximately the same diameter. Then we cut them all the same length with the saw and placed them horizontally on the temple floor. We had to move them around so they fit tightly together. Just as the last board was in place, we heard the familiar *splat* of our afternoon rain.

As the rain fell with increasing intensity, Master Akio scurried around the temple checking the roof and walls for leaks. When the rain passed, he declared, "We build good temple! No water come in."

I looked at Master Akio, rubbing my stomach. "Is it just me or are you hungry too?"

He flashed me his impish, little boy grin. "I'm starved!"

"Are we done for the day?"

Master Akio looked around the temple and then took a quick peek outside. He turned to me and said, "Not done. We pile wood and palm fronds."

It took us less than ten minutes to pile the excess materials and pick up all our tools. Even so, I was going to have to find the lantern tonight because we were going to be cooking in the dark.

When we arrived back at the camp, Master Akio turned to me, "Master Cook, what surprise you have in magic supplies to make quick supper?"

I went to the supplies containers to get the lantern and dig out my emergency supply of mac and cheese. Even though I brought lots and lots of food, I still packed two boxes for emergencies.

I had the trusty lantern lit and dinner cooking on the stove in record time. I glanced up from my culinary tasks toward the beach and was surprised to see Master Akio lying on his back in the sand. He was using the backpack as a pillow and he appeared to be staring out at the ocean.

The tea was ready, but the macaroni was still gently boiling, so I took Master Akio his drink. He smiled at me as he moved into an upright position to accept the cup I handed him. "Graham, we build great temple. You work hard. Your skill get better. I work hard also. Skill is pretty good. Body is very tired. I forget I am old man now. Sorry I not help cook supper."

"That's okay. I hope I have half the energy you have when I am your age."

Master Akio grinned, "You have to live that long first."

I walked back towards the stove, thinking supper should be ready. Part way there I hollered back, "I've got a great teacher. He'll help keep me alive."

"Your teacher good, not miracle worker." I chuckled out loud as I dished out our dinner.

177

I handed Master Akio his first bowl of macaroni and cheese. He looked at it, paused for a moment to offer a quick blessing and then took a tentative nibble on the pasta. With the deft skill of a master surgeon, Master Akio maneuvered a huge heaping spoonful of pasta into his mouth.

I looked over with shock and horror at the frantic pace Master Akio was shoveling in his food. This was the first time I had ever seen him lose his sense of decorum and manners. He could see the shocked or disturbed look on my face. He simply grinned and said, "What?"

In my confusion I responded, "Would you like a bigger spoon?"

"Yes, please!"

I got up and grabbed the biggest serving spoon we had. He took the spoon from me with a hearty, "Thank you!"

After a few minutes of witnessing his manic feeding frenzy, I had to turn away. I couldn't stand to look at the way he was eating. As I turned away, Master Akio spoke. "Graham, your shorts on tight?"

I turned back toward Master Akio with an appalled and perplexed look, "No! And why would you ask that?"

He grinned. He had noodles plastered all over his face. I think there were even a few in his hair. He looked like a toddler with their first piece of cake. It was rather disgusting.

Master Akio could tell I was checking out his hair. He pointed to his head and asked, "Here?"

I responded with an exasperated, "Yes."

"Good."

"Good? What do you mean good?"

Master Akio's tone of voice turned from glee to scolding, "Yes, good! Graham, your shorts on tight. You worry what is proper and what is not. We are only two people on island. No one see. Graham, life is to be lived and sometimes that mean not do what people think is proper. Sometimes eat food with..." he tugged on his hair, obviously not sure of the word, and continued, "Is good. Babies wear food, because experience food with whole body not just..." he pointed to his mouth. "Food is to experience."

With unbelievable speed he reached into my plate and grabbed a handful of pasta. Before I could even think to stop him, he smeared pasta in my hair and then down across my face.

In anger I jumped up and back. In my agitated state this didn't go very well for me. My sudden movement collapsed my makeshift bench causing the logs to roll backwards. I was knocked over, landed on the bench, then tumbled and landed face first into the sand. Not one of my finer or most graceful moments.

I slowly stood back up, checking to see if anything was hurt from my potentially dangerous tumble, grumbling all the while. Now I had mac and cheese and sand in my hair. What remained of my dinner was now strewn all over the beach.

Master Akio looked at me with concern in his eyes, "You okay, Graham?"

As soon as I confirmed I was not hurt, Master Akio collapsed in fits of hysterical laughter.

Despite my utter sense of indignation, I found it really hard to stay mad at someone whose complete essence was consumed with fits of gleeful, body-wracking convulsions of laughter.

Soon I was laughing almost as hard as he was. Of course, dumping the rest of our meal on top of his head did help me get into the mood. I briefly thought about getting out some pudding as well, but decided I didn't really want to waste dessert.

That night I got the lesson that I, Graham Alexander Connelly, take myself a little too seriously, or as Master Akio says, my underwear is a little too tight.

A brilliant metaphor popped into my head. Go commando - don't wear underwear - so your underwear doesn't bunch up and give you grief. Which simply means, have fewer expectations about how things are to be. Let go and allow!

Day Twenty-Two

It was just starting to get light inside the tent. I rolled over in my cot and looked towards Master Akio. He was asleep with small bits of mac and cheese mushed in his hair. I guess our late night wash in the ocean wasn't completely successful. I smiled at the absurdity of last night's lesson in how I am and how I appear to others.

I stood up very quietly, being careful not to wake Master Akio. My side hurt slightly when I moved. I assumed it was from all the laughing the night before. I bent down to get a clean shirt out of my duffle bag, and heard Master Akio chuckle. "Morning, Graham. You still wear your supper."

"Good morning, Master Akio. I don't mean to be the bearer of bad news, but so are you."

Master Akio smiled. "We need real wash today, huh?" As he stood up he grimaced slightly. "Your side hurt also?" he asked.

"Yes," I said as I rubbed my ribs lightly.

"That sign of great day when side hurts from laugh!"

We cleaned up as quickly as we could to beat the inferno that was rapidly building inside the tent. We completed just as the heat was becoming unbearable; it was a relief when we unzipped the tent and stepped into the fresh air and went to our seats to start our morning routine. I chuckled, remembering what a production it was to rebuild my bench. It seemed that every time we had a major piece put back together, one of us fell down in the sand laughing. It took forever to rebuild the bench. Master Akio must have sensed what I was chuckling about because he turned to me and said, "Bench is okay."

We both chuckled out loud as we settled in to our spots. I sat as straight as I could and began my meditation with the slow deep breathing I had now become quite good at. I focused all my attention on my breathing. As I slowly exhaled, I felt myself slip effortlessly and quickly into a deep, peaceful, meditative calm.

I felt truly at peace while I meditated. At least I thought it was peace; I had never really experienced it before. Or had I? Did I experience peace while I was out on my quest?

I didn't know how long I'd been meditating, but I knew it was over when I started asking questions, instead of just having them arise. Perhaps it was the smell of Master Akio cooking breakfast that brought me back to the island.

I opened my eyes. Master Akio was no longer sitting beside me. I could hear him chopping something in the kitchen. I got up to see what he was up to. As he noticed me walking back from the beach he said, "Graham, that was great long meditation. I talk to you - you hear me?"

I was slightly taken aback. "You talked to me?"

"Yes, I talk to you. I ask you if you want to lead stretches. You no answer. I think you not listen because you not want to exercise. Then I ask what you want for food and you not answer. I knew you deep in meditation. You always answer about food."

I laughed and tried my best to sound hurt and annoyed, "What do you mean I always respond to food?"

He grinned. "Breakfast almost ready. You get bowls?"

I moved closer and nonchalantly asked, "What's for breakfast?"

"Porridge."

Actually it turned out to be porridge, tinned fruit, orange juice, coffee, and tea. The orange juice was a real treat, even though it was warm.

I carried Master Akio's juice and tea to his chair and then returned to fill two bowls with steaming hot porridge. I handed Master Akio his porridge and then sat down next to him. Before I ate my first bite, I took a few moments to gaze out into the blue expanse of the ocean. Once again, it was a beautiful morning in paradise.

Master Akio turned and faced me with a serious expression on his face. "Graham, what you see out there? You always stop and look out at ocean before you eat."

I turned to look him directly in the eyes. "Really? I was aware I did that some of the time, but I didn't realize I did it all the time."

He smiled. "What you see, Graham?"

I sat there for a long time, perplexed and unable to answer. Every time I thought I could express my thoughts, they just got lost between my brain and my vocal cords. I tried four or five times to speak and just couldn't.

Master Akio could see my painfully tortured expressions. He changed his tone and spoke to me as one would expect a very kind and wise old man to do, "Idea too big for words. Sometimes more words bad. Many books, hundreds of pages long, written on love. Everyone know what mean when you say love someone, but if I ask you say what love is, you now want write hundreds of pages. Graham, you shorts too tight! You make simple thing more difficult. When you look out at ocean, what you see?"

I smiled and opened my mouth to speak but a huge lump instantly formed deep inside my throat. I could feel it, the words were right there, right on the tip on my tongue. I wanted to scream, but I was hopelessly unable to. I could not say what I wanted and needed to. I felt tears well up in my eyes and felt swallowed by a feeling that I was inconsequential. It overwhelmed me. Tears began to stream down my face, and with the tears came freedom for my voice. I croaked, "Small. So very, very small."

Master Akio smiled, slowly nodding his head. He spoke in a whisper, "I know! When I come to this island I sick many days after many days in boat. One day I okay. I think I need warn Japan about America. I look at ocean many, many days. I look for way to warn Japan or to fight America. Many months I live on beach with little food and no house. One day after meditation, I see I small in ocean of life. Things not important. Most important, what I do for people. No people with me. I need do what right for me."

I interrupted Master Akio, "Could you please explain that more for me?"

"Graham, I build house and temple. When I build house in Japan, I no like work, I send builder home and get better builder. But Akio is only builder - bad builder and better builder. I choose what builder Akio be every day and every time I build something. I choose be better builder for everything. Some days hard because Akio do everything and no one see it. Only Akio see it. Graham, I work many, many days. I choose be better builder in all life - for Akio, not for other people."

My tears continued as I listened, enraptured by what Master Akio was saying. My heart was ripping wide open. I found it absolutely amazing that, while he could have allowed his aloneness to turn him into a bitter old man, he chose a different path. Master Akio discovered what Sara would have called enlightenment. I smiled with the realization that Buddha found enlightenment under a Bodhi tree, and my friend, teacher, and Master found enlightenment on an island.

"What you smile for, Graham?"

"Master Akio, the Buddha found enlightenment under a Bodhi tree, you found enlightenment on an island."

Master Akio cocked his head to one side. I could tell he was thinking about my words. With a smile and a deep breath he exclaimed, "You surprise Akio, you American dog! You know about Buddha? Japanese teach Akio that American religion is money."

I chuckled, "To some degree, that is true, but right now my country is going through a spiritual awakening. Many people are questioning who they are and why they are here. They are looking at other cultures for answers."

"Graham, I make steps to be more like Buddha, but I not like Buddha. I not find what you call enlightenment." He flashed me one of his mischievous grins. "Please, I tell you more now. Graham, no one tell me what good or not good. Only I choose what good or not good. Father teach me this. He make paper and only send paper he think good to Emperor. Emperor not say what good paper. Father say what good paper. Graham, you crash plane because you not choose to be best. You say ok is good." He nodded his head. "It is perfect."

It was now my turn to look puzzled. "How can you say that it was, or is, perfect that I crashed my plane and almost killed Blaine?'

"Think, Graham. Before you crash plane, you want come to island with no people?"

"No! Well, not without a boat load of women by my side."

Master Akio laughed. "Before you crash plan you plan to do meditation and write in journal?"

"No!"

"Is Blaine better co-pilot now?"

I smiled. "Yes, he is."

Master Akio used his grandfatherly voice again, "Graham, Universe is teacher and we all here to learn lessons. Universe give us gentle lessons. If we not learn lessons it give more hard lessons. Graham, you not listen. Universe or God say, "Ok. We crash Graham plane, almost kill him and Blaine. See if he learn lessons we teach since Graham born." It is perfect because you see! You now work to learn lessons."

I looked at Master Akio, "Don't you think that almost dying is a bit of a harsh way to learn a lesson?"

Master Akio looked at me, his face becoming very soft and sad, "Graham, some people not learn lessons before dying."

He stood up, "Finish porridge." Then he saw my bowl. "Oh! Start eat porridge!" He turned and took his dishes back to the kitchen. I was so engrossed in the conversation that I had forgotten to eat. That was the first time conversation ever got between me and food! The cold porridge was not very good.

After cleaning up camp, we did our morning stretches and I did my morning run. Even though it was all a little off our usual schedule we still went through all our morning activities. After my run, we took soap and shampoo and went into the ocean to wash the noodles out of our hair.

Once we were clean, Master Akio turned to me, "Bring your offering and journal. We go to our temple." In a few minutes, we had both collected our offerings, some water and my journal and were on our way up the beach.

It felt a little odd to go to the temple without a backpack full of tools. We had been working so hard, and now it was done. Today we were in no hurry; it was like we were out for a stroll.

We stopped in front of the temple and set the water down. I just stood there staring in awe. I had never built anything from start to finish with my hands. I did help Blaine build his deck, but that was only for an afternoon, so I didn't really finish it.

Master Akio was not wearing shoes, so he just brushed off his feet before entering. I had to take my shoes off first. It suddenly occurred to me that on my next trip I was bringing flip flops for me and Master Akio.

I quietly entered the temple just in time to see Master Akio break into his happy dance. He continued to dance and excitedly asked, "This feel great?"

I couldn't help but laugh and grin, "Yes, it does!"

"Graham, you move in temple and find lucky spot where you want hang offering."

"Okay." I started to slowly walk around inside the temple.

Master Akio playfully scolded me, "No! No! You need dance Happy Dance, not walk. You will find magic spot when feet feel heavy – you cannot move from spot."

I looked over to Master Akio in mild shock and deep confusion, "Master Akio, this is a temple. Are we not supposed to be serious? We definitely should not be dancing."

Master Akio stopped. "Graham, many temples in world for long time where people dance and have fun. This our temple. We say we want temple to be fun. Temple is fun and serious." A mischievous smile flashed across his face. "Temple also keep water out." He returned to his dance. "Graham, this our temple, so we make it any way we want. Be happy."

I gave Master Akio a tentative smile that said, "Okay. I don't understand this at all, but I'll do as I'm told." I slowly started dancing the Graham Alexander Connelly version of a happy dance. I was so self-conscious. But as I stopped focusing on how I looked and started feeling my way through the space, I let go. Or, as Master Akio would say, I loosened my shorts. I was soon leaping around and jumping up and down. I felt like I was driven by some magical force. We danced our tribal happy dances for a long time. I could feel the sweat pour down the middle of my back and my face.

I had been dancing in the same spot for quite a while before I realized it. Yup! Master Akio was right! My legs didn't want to move and they felt very heavy. My magic spot was on the wall to the left of the entrance. I looked around and saw that Master Akio wasn't dancing any more. Rather, he was swaying back and forth to some internal drum. He was standing in front of the wall directly in front of the entrance. I stopped dancing. Soon Master Akio stopped swaying and turned to me, his face glistening with sweat.

"That was fun," I sheepishly admitted to Master Akio.

He grinned and agreed, "Yes, it was." He walked over to where I was standing and asked, "This your lucky spot?"

"Yes!"

We spent about half an hour figuring out how to fix my small piece of paper to the wall. Finally, it was decided that we would build a small frame to hold my writing and then lash the frame to one of the middle support beams. Since our upper walls were hinged to drop down, we couldn't attach it to them. For Master Akio's offering of his practice sword, we decided it would be best if we built a small shelf and lashed it to the support post closest to his magic spot.

We gathered our offerings and exited the temple. We both selected the wood we thought we'd need from the pile and then returned to camp for lunch and to build our small projects.

Since we were both really eager to start our projects, lunch was pretty much a non-event. Normally, food was a big thing with me, but I was happy with just a brief break to heat a tin of soup and bake a few biscuits in the cast iron stew pot, which worked great as an oven, so we could get right into our work.

I was able to build the small wooden frame, but Master Akio had to show me how to do the spiral lashing to hold the parchment in place. I practiced on a small stick and a scrap piece of paper. Thanks to the lessons in weaving the grass mats, this spiral weaving seemed rather easy to do, once I understood the process. I was just putting the finishing touches on my frame when Master Akio came over to check on my progress. "You finish?"

I looked up. "Yes, I am all done."

Master Akio examined my frame and smiled. "Very good!"

Since it was still early afternoon, I asked if we were going to hang them today.

Master Akio smiled and said, "Yes, but I not use sword after hang in temple. I want use one more time. Get your sword."

I felt like a kid who just got money for an ice cream. Carefully, I put my frame down, leapt off my chair, and excitedly scampered off to get my sword. I had stopped carrying it while we were building the temple. I returned just a few moments later. Master Akio had moved down the beach to where we could swing our swords without fear of breaking things. I could feel my heart pounding a million beats a second. I loved sword fighting.

As I ran towards Master Akio, I could see his sword in his rope belt. When I got close, I stopped to hang my sword on my belt as well.

He smiled and then bowed. I bowed as well. Neither of us took our eyes off the other, watching every move. After bowing, we stood and drew our swords. We slowly raised our swords over our heads, both at the ready. Master Akio was waiting for me to strike first and I was waiting for him.

He shuffled to the right. In my exuberance, I panicked and swung first. It was high. Master Akio smiled, blocked, and then countered with a mid-thigh swing. I parried and stepped back, raising my sword in defense. He shuffled forward and then launched into a long series of attacks. I was able to counter them all and even managed to get him on the defensive for a few moments at a time. I was holding my own and I wasn't pressing too hard. I felt pretty good about my abilities.

Master Akio swung for a mid-waist strike. I lowered my sword, waiting for the resounding crack that our swords would inevitably make as they crashed together, but his sword swung harmlessly past mine. I smiled, thinking that the danger had passed and he had just missed a blow because he was tired. I even considered easing up when he nimbly leapt forward and thrust. I feebly tried to defend myself, but my grip was wrong. I had the right grip for a slash to the waist but not for this sudden attack. The blow connected with my stomach with a thud, knocking the breath right out of me. I faltered, gasping and wheezing for air. Master Akio instantly reversed the direction of his sword and sung again, smashing my sword right out of my hands.

I had lost the match. I was left gasping for air, without my sword. To the best of my winded ability, I bowed to Master Akio. He bowed to me, then moved to stand next to me, concern on his face, "You okay?"

I tried to smile but it came out as a grimace. "Just winded," I feebly said. "That was a really great move."

Master Akio was still looking at me, distress deep in his eyes. "Sorry. Not mean to hit hard."

After about three or four minutes I was finally able to take in a full breath. I could almost smile. "No worries, Master Akio. It was a great lesson. I realized that I don't know everything about sword fighting so I need to be a lot more aware."

Master Akio walked over to where my sword had landed and picked it up. He handed it to me. "Good fight?" he asked.

"Yes."

"I see you smile. I think you know what I do, so I push harder."

"I was smiling because I thought you were getting tired and I was thinking of taking it easy on you!"

"Very funny. We both think we are right, but we both are wrong. I think you know what I do and you think you know what I do. So what you think lesson is, Graham?"

I chuckled, "That's easy. Don't trust you with a sword!"

Master Akio grinned, "Yes, that one lesson, but what bigger lesson?"

I didn't answer right away. We both started walking towards the kitchen. Once we arrived I said, "I think the lesson is not to make assumptions and to always stay focused.

"What 'assumption'?"

I thought to myself, "Excellent question, Master Akio. What are assumptions?" Bit by bit I gathered my thoughts. "Assumptions are judgments we make based on past history or past behaviour. It is like me bringing you tea every night because you had tea the night before and the night before and the night before, without me asking you if you would like tea."

"Ah. I understand this word 'assumption'. I make assumption sun rise every morning and set every night and I make assumption Graham always hungry."

I smiled, "Yes, those are good assumptions."

"Bad thing with assumption – we not think about choices. Today, you not ask if I tired. You make assumption I tired." He paused, then added, "We go to temple to meditate on this word assumption after we honour temple with offerings."

I readily agreed to go and Master Akio suggested we wash up first. By now we were both comfortable with him going through my clothes and picking out what he would like to wear without asking. At first, it felt very strange to share my clothes and toiletries with Master Akio. I had always been very protective of what was mine. I never liked sharing; I worked too hard to earn money and gather possessions. I was now okay with it - although I was really glad I brought two tooth brushes. *Why did I bring two tooth brushes?* I wondered.

I smiled and muttered to myself, "Hmm, I wonder how much of this packing extra food and things was the Universe providing me - or us - for this very situation?" I snorted. *Great! More things to think about.*

Master Akio playfully yelled at me, "You come to temple or you talk to self all day?"

"Both."

"Both? You like old person. Always talk to self."

I carefully picked up my now-framed offering and a bottle of water and started walking up the beach. I turned and looked back to Master Akio who was hurriedly picking up the mounting rack for his sword. "I am only following the example of my great Master."

He chuckled, "No! You not learn from me or you talk to self in Japanese!"

We teased and playfully bantered back and forth as we walked on the beach toward the temple. The walk passed quickly and before we knew it, we were there.

Before entering, we both paused; me to take off my shoes and Master Akio to brush off his feet. We entered the temple and both went to the center to sit down.

"Graham, I tell you some things here. This our temple so we make ceremony not very serious, but need be like Mother Earth."

"You mean sacred?"

"Yes, that word. I forget how to say it, but yes! That word."

"Sacred," I repeated.

"I make ceremony sacred but also teach you things you use at home." Master Akio looked at me inquisitively, "That good?"

I nodded my head in agreement, "Yes, that is very good."

Master Akio smiled. "Graham, everything is energy and everything is spirit. All things come from spirit energy and all things return to spirit energy. Energy is in five groups - earth, water, air, fire, and spirit. All energy can change to other energy groups. All energy uses other energy to live. Tree is earth energy. When we burn tree, fire energy mix with air energy and turn tree to spirit energy. If no want to burn tree, water energy can stop fire. People are earth energy but need

197

air, water, and fire energy to live. Air to breathe, water to drink, fire from sun to warm, and earth energy to provide us with the food we eat. Need all energies to live. Today in ceremony we thank all energies of life."

Master Akio began taking things out of his pockets: matches, a small candle, a water bottle, and what looked like a small piece of a hand-woven palm mat. He placed all the items on the floor between us and looked deeply into my eyes.

"Graham, all around us and all inside us is spirit. All we can see and all we can dream is spirit. We all spirit. Your spirit is in me and my spirit is in you. When I understand you are me and I am you, I not hate Americans for killing my friends, for destroy my life. I not hate anyone. I not hate Akio."

His voice changed and he looked around the temple. "Akio understand Akio is spirit and spirit is this temple. Akio bless this temple and ask spirit of this temple to honour and bless Akio."

He looked at me and said, "Now you."

I sputtered, "Pardon? You want me to say something?"

He nodded, "Yes, say something like I say. What you say is perfect. Say from heart."

I paused and took a few moments to think, trying to remember what Master Akio had just said. I took a big breath and spoke, "I am one with the Universe. I come from Spirit and Spirit comes from me. I am connected to all and all is connected to me. There is no separation between me and Spirit.

We are one and the same. I am all things and all possibilities. I ask the energy of Spirit, which is the possibility of all possibilities, to bless and watch over this temple."

Master Akio looked at me with a small tear in his eye. "Very beautiful, Graham."

I looked at him and shrugged my shoulders. "I don't know where that came from! I have never said anything like that before. I have no idea where the words came from. They were not my words."

Master Akio grinned and spoke softly, "Words from Spirit. Spirit is all things. Not your words. Spirit say words from you."

I paused to consider his words before asking, "Those were words from Spirit and Spirit spoke through me?"

He nodded and then carried on with our ceremony by asking for a blessing for our temple from each of the elements - earth, water, fire, and air. He then asked me to offer a blessing from each of the elements as well. Every time I offered my blessing, words came through me - words that I would never have dreamed of uttering. After my initial shock and disbelief wore off, the blessings became easier and easier.

Finally, it was time to hang our offerings. Master Akio turned to me. "Say sacred words and hang offering."

I picked up my offering and held it for a few moments. I didn't know what to say. Nothing was coming to me or through me this time, so I decided to read the words I had written as my offering out loud. "To the Universe, I don't fully understand you yet. I know you have placed Master Akio in my life. I know you have given me a past; why that past I don't know. I also don't know what my future holds, but I am open to having it unfold before me and with me. I am open to you."

I paused and reflected for a few seconds on the words I had written so many days ago. I stood up and walked over to the post to lash my offering to it. Once it was in place, I just stood there for a few minutes looking at my offering before returning to my spot.

Master Akio took hold of his practice sword. He held his offering for many moments before he broke the silence. "This sword is symbol for strength, learning, and friendship. This sword is tool we use for first lessons as master and student. Start of many lessons together. This wood is strong, like our friendship and our love. I thank Universe for guide us together. This symbol hang in temple many years."

He reached over and grabbed the rack that was to hold the sword on the wall. He stood up and walked over to the other post, tying the rack in place. Once the rack was secure, he reached down, picked up the sword and carefully placed it onto the rack. He stepped back and bowed to the sword. When he turned to face me, I could see small tears rolling down his face. "Graham, Akio old man. I have two things - this sword and war sword. When I pass to other side and return to Spirit energy you are to have both swords."

I was stunned; I was incapable of saying anything.

Master Akio wiped his tears away with his hand. He smiled and said, "Now we meditate."

Since I was unable to say anything, I just nodded in agreement, closed my eyes, and began to breathe in. I soon found myself floating in that familiar, giant, black sea of nothingness that was also boundless and endless in possibilities.

I felt a change in the temple temperature as the rain suddenly pounded down on our temple and I knew the sun would soon start its daily decent. Ever so slowly, I opened my eyes. I quietly stood, my legs tingling and aching in protest. They were still not used to me sitting cross-legged for so long. I was trying not to disturb Master Akio. As I stood upright, he spoke, "Your meditations get much longer. Very good!"

I smiled and simply said, "Thank you."

Master Akio flashed me one of his impish, little boy grins as he stood up. "Want to go fishing?"

I frowned. "I have taught you all I know about fishing."

He laughed. "I starve to death if you teach everything to know about fishing."

"The only way you are going to get any better, I guess, is for you to practice. I have seen you fish. You need lots of practice."

We continued our bragging and teasing all the way back to camp.

After we'd each caught a fish, we swam around and played in the ocean before deciding it was time for supper. It was a simple meal of rice, fish, and tinned beans, plus our usual coffee and tea.

It didn't really take long for us to clean up afterward, so we had extra time to just sit around the fire. I got up to put another log on when Master Akio asked, "We have sweets?"

I smiled. "Yes, we have more cookies. Would you like some?"

Even without seeing Master Akio's face, I could hear the smile in his voice, "Yes, please!"

I brought the cookies and some fresh tea for Master Akio. I also topped up my coffee before settling down at the fire again. "Master Akio, I have a few questions for you."

Master Akio looked up from the flames. He had a mouthful of cookies, so I continued, "I am leaving in eight days. I have lots of food and equipment. Would you like some of it?" I paused for a moment and I'm sure my face looked serious. "I don't know what to do, Master Akio. Do we let Captain Taka know about you and take the supplies to your beach? Or, do we carry the supplies you want to your home by ourselves? Do we let people know about you or not?"

Master Akio did not respond for a very long time and I did not push him for an answer. With a heavy sigh, he finally spoke, "Graham, I say before I have no one in Japan. Japan I remember not Japan now. This island home now. If people know Akio here, no peace for Akio or Graham!"

He paused for just a moment then passionately continued, "Graham, Akio blood Japanese, Akio family Japanese and Akio body Japanese, but Akio not Japanese now. Akio spirit of Universe. If people know Akio live, people want Akio be Japanese. To be Japanese not bad – it good – but I not Japanese now. Akio old man, alone many years. Akio man with no country! Graham, I want die on this island. This my home, my country. Seven days we say good bye. On eighth day, I go to Old House and you stay here. Boat come and take you to Hawaii. When you come back, you come here to Summer House so no one know I here."

Once again, he paused briefly, "I answer question now. Yes, I like have things you want leave. We need carry to Old House."

I had a huge lump in my throat at the thought of leaving Master Akio. I could only muster, "You can have whatever you want."

Master Akio replied with a subdued, "Thank you."

We both sat in silence staring at the fire, lost in our own thoughts, unable - or unwilling - to speak. Finally, Master Akio broke the silence,   "You have many pages in journal to write on?"

"Not many."

"That bad and good. Good you write much, bad not many pages. I make good paper for you. Tomorrow we go to Old House. We take food and other things. We sleep there. Come back to Summer House next day." Master Akio got up. "I tired. I got to bed. Good night, Graham." He stopped in the kitchen to wash and put away his cup before he went to bed.

I sat staring at the fire for many hours, trying to figure out what to do. I knew I was coming back, but for how long and when? I had already used up all my holidays to be here. I had the money to fly back. Should I sell my condo and buy a condo on the beach? How could I even start to tell people about my adventure here? When I could not stop yawning, with no answers and nothing resolved, I went to bed.

Day Twenty-Three

I woke with a start. The heat in the tent was unbearable. I could feel the sweat pouring down my back and pooling in all the recesses of my body. I had overslept and the heat of the day was driving me out. When, I turned to wish Master Akio a good morning, he was not there. Apparently, he got up quietly and left me to sleep.

I got up and quickly changed my clothes to flee the sauna. As I unzipped the tent, I spied Master Akio meditating on his chair. I zipped the tent behind me and quietly joined him. I began my daily mediation ritual. Soon I was lost, deep in the void.

I felt and heard Master Akio stand. I opened my eyes and greeted him with a cheerful, "Good Morning."

He cheerfully replied back, "Good morning. We stretch and then you run. I make us breakfast.

As I returned from my run, I noticed Master Akio hadn't finished preparing breakfast. I walked into the kitchen thinking I could help. He looked up from his chopping and smiled. He was cutting up the last of our potatoes and onions. "Graham, you journal. I finish breakfast."

"Okay. But are you sure you don't need any help?"

Master Akio resumed his chopping. "No thank you. You journal."

206

With my journal, ink, and pen in hand, I sat down on my bench. I gazed out at the magnificent ocean. I never grew tired of watching the waves roll onto the shore, or the tiny sand crabs being swept onto the shore or out into the ocean.

I opened the bottle of ink, dipped my pen in and put sacred pen to paper.

Day 23

For the first time in my life I can say that I am truly, truly happy. These last few days have been eye and heart opening and, at times, heart wrenching. The happiness I am experiencing on the island is leading me to question my life back in what I previously called 'home'... even my very existence. I have to go back to Hawaii, but this island feels more like a home than my condo.

I know I came back to the island to search for who I was. I really thought I would discover that I needed to learn to fly the big planes or fly for the rich and famous; that I needed a Porsche or a Ferrari and a bigger house. Maybe I needed a couple girl friends in different cities scattered across multiple countries.

*Now my search seems to revolve
around what I can get rid of so I
can spend more time with family
and friends...*

I snorted out loud. Blaine and Sara were my friends, but the longer I stayed on this island the more like family they became to me. Caring about others was a really strange feeling to the old self-serving, self-absorbed Graham. I had pushed people away for so long that it felt really bizarre to actually want to pull people into my life. The very thought of allowing someone to get to know me scared the heck out of me. But it was extremely exhilarating at the same time.

"Breakfast is cooked, come eat," Master Akio called. I put my pen down, secured the lid on the bottle of ink, closed my journal, and carefully carried them all back to the table.

I savored the last of the potatoes and onions. From here on in, we were eating dry or tinned goods, with the exceptions of the fish we caught and the fresh vegetables from Master Akio's garden.

I took Master Akio's tea and his plateful of food to his seat, before grabbing my coffee and plate of food. Master Akio put the dishwater on the stove to heat and then we walked over to our respective chairs.

As I sat on my makeshift bench, I looked out at the vast horizon of crystal blue waters and was surprised to see a smoke trail from a ship on the distant horizon. "I wonder where that ship is going," I said while scooping up a huge forkful of my favourite breakfast.

"Many hours, many days I look for ship and not see on water."

Over breakfast we talked about current trading between Japan and the United States and the excellent quality of Japanese cars.

As we washed up and put away the dishes, I continued telling Master Akio about Japanese and American relations, as best I could remember them. When we were done, I turned to Master Akio and asked, "What food would you like me to leave you and how do we get it to your house?"

Master Akio appeared slightly puzzled, so I continued, "Master Akio, the food we don't eat before I leave I would take off the island and give away. If you want or need anything, you can have it. I bought all this food and I was not planning on taking it back to Hawaii with me. I was going to give it away to Captain Taka or someone on Kwajalein Island."

"You give me food?"

"Yes. Whatever you want, you can have."

We spent the better part of an hour leisurely going through the food supplies. It was fun examining what each item was, determining whether or not Master Akio had eaten it before, and comparing our thoughts on what things tasted like. In the end, he wanted the rice, tea, tinned fruit, cookies, and the flour.

Master Akio grinned, "I eat like a king when you gone! All this food you give me and my garden, I not be hungry again."

I smiled. "Yes, and when I come back I will bring more tea and whatever else you would like me to bring."

Master Akio looked at me in absolute amazement, "You bring more food?"

I grinned, "Yes, when I come back I will bring you different kinds of vegetable seeds - vegetables that you may have never heard of or tasted before. I can bring you enough tea, rice, and cookies to have them every single day for the rest of your life."

Master Akio flashed me one of his impish, little boy grins, "I have cookies and tea every day?"

"Yes, Master Akio, you can have tea and cookies every day."

I noticed a small tear gently roll down his face. He spoke in a whisper, "I miss many things on this island, but I miss most my family and tea. Tea every day be good."

Master Akio was quiet for a few moments, lost in his own thoughts. Then he simply shrugged his shoulders as a way of changing his mood and said to me, "We have time. We take food to Old House, clean garden, and come back here for supper." He shook his head, "Garden big mess."

"I'll get the backpack."

"I get water."

I frantically rummaged around in the sweltering heat of the tent for my camera. I had lived 23 days on the island and had taken no pictures yet. Today was the day. Besides, pictures might help me explain things to Blaine and Sara. Without pictures, I'm pretty sure they would lock me up in a mental institute.

I pictured the conversation now. Blaine asks me, "So, Graham, how was your time alone on the island?"

I would say something like, "Thanks for asking Blaine, but I wasn't alone. On day three I met this Japanese World War II Veteran who taught me to sword fight. I now call him Master and we built a temple together."

About that time, Blaine would be picking up the phone to call for an ambulance to have me sent to a hospital for observation.

I found my camera, grabbed my GPS and the backpack, and quickly fled the tent, barely turning around to zip it closed. I ran over and met Master Akio in the kitchen. He was waiting with the water. I quickly loaded the bottles and all of the rice into the backpack; it was almost full. I only brought a relatively small day pack, as it never occurred to me that I would need to haul large quantities of food five or six miles. I chuckled to myself, "Sheesh, what was I thinking?" I slipped the backpack over my shoulders and turned to Master Akio. "Ready to go?"

Master Akio nodded his head, "Yes, we go." Despite the fact that we wanted to get there and back in one day, we took our time walking the beach. We watched small crabs scurry across the sand; we threw coconuts into the surf; we simply enjoyed the journey.

When we arrived at Master Akio's house we each took off our shoes before going in. We went directly to the kitchen. We stood there, puzzling over where to put the rice. His house was very neat and tidy, so the bugs wouldn't get into the rice, but he had no shelves or any place to store things in his kitchen. After turning around in about five times, he grinned and said, "I need build shelf while you gone. Now I have project to keep busy."

"Yes, you can do that - or we can make one before I go?"

"If we have time. Now put rice there." He pointed to the corner. I slipped the back pack off and took out the rice, placing it in the spot he indicated.

"Now what?"

"You journal. I pick from garden to make lunch. After lunch we clean garden and swim."

"I would love to journal, but I didn't bring it with me. There was no room in the back pack."

Master Akio grinned, "Ok, you meditate now. Go sit by pool. I bring food."

I shrugged my shoulders, "Are you sure I can't help?"

"Yes."

Even though I felt like I was abandoning Master Akio, I left the kitchen, put on my shoes and walked down to the pool. I carefully selected a spot in the shade and sat down on the ground. This ground was harder than the sand at the Summer House. I wondered how I would fare meditating on the hard ground. I closed my eyes and began to focus on my breathing. Breathe in slow and deep, hold, breath out slowly.... Breathe in. . . . Breathe out....

Deeply lost in my meditation, I felt like I was in a place with huge rolling hills of luscious green grass. I could feel and smell the dampness in the air. It was like a picture perfect postcard from Scotland. At any moment, I expected William Wallace to come screaming over the next rise.

I heard the scrunch of footsteps coming from in front of me. I looked intently as the shape of a person slowly materialized from behind the distant hill. First the head, then shoulders, and then arms. The rest of the body followed. The person appeared to be carrying something. There was something vaguely familiar about their gait; I knew this person from somewhere.

I smiled, and as I did, the hills faded into the lush green of my tropical island. The cool dampness of my meditation returned to the muggy and sticky humidity. I opened my eyes to see Master Akio round a corner on the path carrying food.

I tried to move my legs. I felt the painful, prickly sensation of blood trying to return to my limbs. I had successfully put my legs to sleep during my meditation. I tried to move, but my legs had a mind of their own and simply refused. They just weren't moving.

I waved to Master Akio. "I'm here! I can't move. I put my legs to sleep."

Master Akio frowned. "Not good." He walked over to where I was sitting and carefully placed the food beside me. He stood directly in front of me, "Graham, this might hurt."

Without waiting for my response, Master Akio gently pushed me back so I was lying flat on my back. With great care, he unfolded my legs, triggering a massive quantity of blood to rush back into my legs. The pain slowly built from pins and needles to excruciating fire shooting all the way up from my toes to my hips. My legs began to involuntarily spasm.

Master Akio moved and sat down beside me, "Stay still few moment. Then move feet… and then legs."

I decided I'd stay lying down. Master Akio smirked, "I did same as you waiting for ship to pass island in beginning. Not good feeling."

Slowly, the spasms stopped and the fire in my legs subsided. I could move my ankles and my feet. My legs felt tired but I was able to move them. I rolled over and sat up, putting my back to a tree. Master Akio smiled. "You be okay?"

"Yes."

"Good. We eat."

He handed me a coconut bowl and then dished a huge mound of lettuce, tomatoes, and carrots topped with a coconut dressing into it. Since he had no forks, I used my fingers to grab a small mouthful. It was simply delicious.

After lunch and clean up, we both took a short nap. Next it was off to the garden. To my untrained eye the garden looked pretty good. But from the sounds of utter disgust that Master Akio made as he wove his way through the rows, I honestly would have thought elephants had trampled the garden, followed by a swarm of locusts, and an infestation of weeds and bugs in biblical proportions. Of course, it was none of those things. It was merely a man with perfectionist tendencies who had spent many hours each day lovingly tending his garden. I could see his pride and joy was in slight disarray after twenty days of neglect.

Master Akio showed me how to thin the carrots and which ones he was going to allow to go to seed, so he would have carrots again. We spent the better part of the afternoon weeding the garden – removing the local grasses and vegetation trying to establish themselves in the rich soil.

I was bending down to pick out a carrot when I remembered my camera. Without saying a word to Master Akio, I left the garden and snuck over to the backpack lying on the ground nearby. I opened the pack, pulled the camera out of its case, turned it on, and walked back into the garden.

A few feet from Master Akio I raised the camera. I framed the picture and then called out to him, "Master Akio, look up." He looked up and I pushed the shutter button. There was a slight click as the camera took my first picture of Master Akio. It was the very first picture I'd taken since arriving on the island.

Master Akio looked at me with a puzzled expression and asked, "What you have?"

I smiled and replied, "A camera."

As I moved towards Master Akio, I switched on my digital camera's view mode. By the time I was standing next to him, the image I had just taken was displayed on the little screen. I turned the camera and pointed towards the screen. "This is the picture I just took."

Master Akio looked at the camera screen and was visibly shocked. He shook his head in disbelief. It was almost incomprehensible to him that he was looking at a picture of himself standing in his garden with no paper, no messy chemicals, and no multiple steps to get the photograph. He looked at me quizzically, "How?"

I frowned as I tried to figure out a way to explain digital cameras. "This is an electronic camera. Much has changed in electronics since you operated a radar station. The biggest change is parts have gotten smaller. Your station was operated on tubes with parts that took up whole rooms to work. With the invention of transistors, radar station parts got smaller. Then

216

micro-chips were invented. This meant that what your radar station did using a whole building, could now be made with a very small box. Micro-chips changed everything. This camera uses and stores information – your picture - on a micro-chip.

"I operate radar station, yes! But never completely understand it all or, if I did, I forget. All I understand you say - big machines get small because of thing called micro-chip."

"Very simply, yes."

"Good. How many pictures can be in this camera?"

"Lots. More than a thousand."

I stood next to Master Akio and held the camera out at arm's length to take our first picture together. It wasn't a bad picture, although we both agreed we looked pretty scruffy as neither of shaved that morning.

I showed Master Akio how to turn the camera on and off, zoom in and out, and how to view the pictures we had taken. He spent a few moments bossing me around as he practiced, "Graham, go stand there and smile. Graham that not smile! Now go stand there."

After each picture he would excitedly turn on the display panel, looking at the picture with awe. The old Graham would have gotten pretty annoyed by all the pictures and all the stopping to look. The new Graham was actually really excited for Master Akio and appreciated his excitement. I couldn't help but really smile for the camera.

Soon, gardening was all but forgotten as we both got caught up in our picture taking frenzy. We took turns taking pictures of each other beside and in the pool, the temple, the garden, and Master Akio's house. Eventually, I figured out the timer and we had to go back and take pictures of us together in each of the areas. It was a fun way to spend the afternoon.

Master Akio was holding the camera, ready to take a picture of me when he felt the familiar splat of our daily rain shower. He slid the camera under his t-shirt and sprinted to his house, which was the closest building.

By the time we made the 200 yard dash into the dry, safe haven of his house we were both completely soaked. Master Akio grinned as he pulled the camera from under his shirt. Miraculously, it was only damp, not soaking wet; his shirt had absorbed most of the water, saving the camera. He went into his paper making area and selected a couple sheets which he used to dry the outside of the camera.

I looked incredulously at Master Akio, "Didn't that paper take a long time to make? Why are you using it to dry off the camera?"

Master Akio looked at me equally baffled. "Graham, not take long time to have someone make camera? You not work long time to buy camera? Not take long time today we take all these pictures?"

Master Akio abruptly stopped talking, the paper dropping from his hands. I felt the energy in the room change.

It was more alive. I saw Master Akio change as well. He suddenly seemed to stand taller, more sure of himself. There was a glow to his face. He seemed more alive.

Master Akio turned and walked toward me. It was like there was electricity in the air. It was exciting but scary at the same time. It was very unnerving. Master Akio stopped two feet in front of me, his dark black eyes piercing right through me. It felt like he was brushing against my very core, my essence. In a blinding flash I knew I had a soul and Master Akio had touched it, or awakened it. I heard the final loud click of a huge, three story-sized lock being opened. I saw the lock crash down on a marble floor with a deafening crack. Then I heard and felt the body-shaking rattling of an equally massive gold chain fall to the marble floor. It landed with an eardrum shattering *crash.*

I was now terrified. Master Akio sensed this because at the very instant my knees started to shake and I wanted nothing more than to turn and bolt, he spoke sharply, "Graham, stand! Stand tall! Graham, smile from your toes."

"What?" was all I could squeak out.

Master Akio smiled. He was radiating pure love and joy. This was really not helping me; it just added to my feeling of fright and my sense of panic. Master Akio, still smiling, said again, "Breathe, Graham, and smile from your toes."

I closed my eyes, desperately trying to focus my attention on my breathing. Ever so slowly, I could feel the awareness of my breath. I could feel the sense of panic begin to ooze out of me. I could hear Master Akio humming. It wasn't words, it was a tone. He just kept saying hummmmmmmmmmmmmmmmmmmm until he paused for a breath. Then he started again. It was very calming and very soothing. He started humming very quietly but slowly got louder and louder with each repetition. It was infectious. I soon joined him. I don't know how long we just stood there humming, "hummmmmmmmmmmmmmmmmmm, hummmmmmmmmmmmmmmmmmmm."

I felt Master Akio's energy shift. I felt his hand on my chest. He took my hand and placed it on his chest. I could feel the old Graham's presence in the back of my mind. He was dying to say something or get involved and interrupt the process. I smiled and continued to hum, "hummmmmmmmm." I could feel the vibrations in Master Akio's chest as he hummed.

I felt Master Akio's energy shift again. I was beginning to understand that every time there was an energy shift, it indicated he was about to do something different.

"Graham, remember when we first meet and we talk about all things sacred?"

"Yes."

"Good. All things sacred, but only sacred because we make them sacred. Graham, we make sword fight lessons sacred, but other people watch, they see two men play with sticks. We make temple together, we make sacred. Other people find island in 50 years. Find temple, see old building. Think maybe play house for children. Graham, everything is sacred but only to people hold it sacred."

My eyes remained close as he continued, "Two lessons I teach you now. Lesson one - Graham is sacred. Lesson two - anything Graham do is sacred. Graham do sacred work for sacred money. What Graham buy with sacred money is sacred. This camera is sacred. Not hold camera sacred, then not hold money sacred, not hold work sacred. Anything you have need be sacred. Anything you do need be sacred. If not be sacred, why you do it? You meditate on this."

Master Akio's tone softened, "Graham, I old man. I think all my friends and family dead. No one to carry my name. Many years pass since I leave Japan. Maybe no papers in Japan say Akio born or live now. Pictures we take with camera say I live, say I matter."

Even with my eyes closed, I could tell Master Akio was now crying as he spoke, "If you never come back to island, if many years pass before you look at camera again, when you see pictures, spirit of Akio be alive. Graham, pictures sacred. You live many years after Akio. Akio's heart want someone to remember Akio. I always want do something and be something big. Graham, my something big is be your friend and teacher."

Tears were now freely streaming down my face as I opened my eyes to look into my teacher's. "Master Akio," I choked out, "I will always remember you, until I take my very last breath. You have taught me so much about life and you have freed my heart from the chains and constrictions I had put on it. You have no fear of ever being forgotten by me or anyone else I come in contact with."

I breathed deeply and continued, "Master Akio, on my next trip back to our island, I would like to bring Blaine."

Master Akio's eyes light up like fireworks. "Really?"

"Yes, really."

Master Akio grinned like a little boy in a toy store with birthday money in his pocket, "You bring more beer, tea, and Blaine?"

I laughed, "Yes, more beer and tea and if I can find them, some history books written in Japanese."

Master Akio exploded forward and grabbed me in a bear hug, jumping up and down in a circle, "Oh, Graham, that great!"

He let go of me and started his happy dance, leaping about the room. After a few moments of dancing, he turned to me and smiled. "Mother be sad. I not act like good Japanese man. Japanese man not dance like fool and not hug other men."

"Master Akio, she may not understand, but she is your mother. She will . . ."

I was instantly transported to the house of my youth. I was twelve years old. It was my birthday. I could see the dingy yellow walls and I could smell the rotting of the house. It was falling down in disrepair all around us, but it was all they could afford. No, it was all my mother could afford.

My father had once again spent his pay check on booze and was yelling at me to get him a beer out of the fridge. I grabbed the beer in a panic and ran into the living room. I tripped over the frayed corner of the carpet, and as I fell the beer flew out of my hand and landed with a crash on the coffee table. The impact caused the beer can to burst, spewing the sticky amber liquid everywhere.

My father exploded in a fit of rage. He grabbed my arm with his left hand and punched me in the body with his right three or four times before my mother could wrestle her way in between us to take the blows. When my father was in a rage, it didn't matter who he beat as long as someone got it.

I slowly inched my broken body out of the room. I could hear my mother's wails as my father turned his full attention to her. I crawled outside and covered my ears. It turned out to be one of the most horrible beatings my father ever inflicted on anyone.

I snapped back to the present and finished my sentence, ". . . she will always love you." I felt my body go limp and crash to the floor.

I awoke to something cold and wet on my forehead. Master Akio was leaning over me with concern all over his face. "You okay, Graham?"

I grimaced. My head hurt. I apparently banged it on the floor when I collapsed.

"You talk, then you stop, talk few more words and fall down. What happen?"

I made a move to get up and Master Akio helped me to a sitting position with a word of caution, "Slow."

"Master Akio, talking about your mother and your mother's love transported me back to my childhood. I was twelve years old. I remembered a horrible incident. I have hated my mother and father for the last 30 years of my life. I felt they were to blame for everything that went wrong in my life. I have not forgiven them for how they were or how they treated me. But now, for the first time in my life, I realize that my mother loved me. I don't know why she stayed with the monster of a man who was my father. I don't understand any of it. For 30 years I carried around bitter resentment that I was unloved and no one cared for me. But in this moment, I know she did."

As I finished my last sentence I was sobbing; whole body wracking sobs of joy and rapture. "Master Akio, my mother loved me!" I jumped up and started to do a happy dance, "My mother actually loved me!" I yelled at the top of my lungs, "My mother loved me!"

Master Akio jumped up and joined my happy dance.

We danced for a very long time. My legs and arms were beginning to tire. Almost in unison we both stopped. Despite the tears and snot all over my face, I grinned at Master Akio. "The rain has stopped. Maybe we should go home."

Master Akio playfully smirked. "I home. You want say Summer Home?"

"Yes, I guess you're right. Let's get our things and go to the Summer Home."

We collected the camera then went out to the garden. We filled the soaking wet backpack with some carrots and lettuce for supper, then I washed my face and we re-filled our water bottles at the pool before beginning the long walk home.

While we walked home, I tried my best to explain to Master Akio the various experiences I had gone through during the day - the sensation of being transported back to my childhood home; the gigantic lock and chain; fainting; realizing I was loved and lovable. Despite reliving some very painful memories, it was a great day. And because I was so engrossed in the conversation, even the walk back home seemed to take only a few moments.

I realized we missed our daily fishing trip. Yet, even without fresh fish for supper, it was still easy to make a meal. I had over-bought supplies for the month. We had salad (or sort of - it was just lettuce and carrots), pasta, and tinned ham.

After washing our dishes and cleaning up the kitchen, we sat around the fire for a while enjoying our coffee, tea, and each other's company. We went off to bed early; it had been a big day.

Days Twenty-Four to Twenty-Eight

The next five days fell into a comfortable routine that made each day blend one into the next.

Every morning we were driven out of the tent by the heat. From there we went to our temple to meditate and followed that with some stretches. We returned to our camp and Master Akio made breakfast while I ran to the temple, back through camp to the Dog Leg and then back to camp. Together, we cleaned up after breakfast.

Each day we took another load of food or equipment to Master Akio's home. Once we unloaded our cargo, we worked in the garden thinning the rows and transplanting the plants that were too close to each other. After a simple lunch, Master Akio sent me off to journal while he made paper. Most days we'd take an afternoon swim and then continue on with our journaling and paper-making.

The afternoon rain would drive me and my journal from the poolside into Master Akio's house.

While it rained we spent time talking about our families and what life was like for each of us growing up. We had shared a few similar experiences. I was always hungry as a child. Master Akio was always hungry during the war and for the first few years he lived on this island, until his garden became self-sufficient and he learned to fish. Master Akio was also an only child and we both came from very small towns.

After the afternoon rain ceased, we walked back to the Summer House, arriving just before dark. Sometimes, if there was still enough light, we would go fishing before cooking supper. After supper we'd do our dishes and then sit around the fire talking before going to bed.

One day I had to weave together some grass to make a belt. I had lost enough weight while on the island that my shorts were falling off, even with the belt I'd brought.

On day 28 we carried the clothes that Master Akio wanted to the Old House. Our walk back to the Summer House was very somber.

Day Twenty-Nine

Once again, I could feel the morning heat building inside the tent. I rolled over and was startled fully awake. Master Akio was already awake, sitting cross-legged on the ground, facing me. "Good Morning Master Akio. Why are you staring at me?"

Master Akio's face changed; he looked quite serious. "Tomorrow last day I see you. Universe send you here. Universe maybe not send you back. I look so I remember you if you not come back."

The old Graham *said Ick! That's gross*. The new Graham was touched by Master Akio's kindness. I could not even fathom what my leaving was going to be like for him. For the first time in 70 years he had company, someone to talk with and do things with – a friend. Just the very thought of what it must be like to go through years of loneliness, only to briefly have company before going back to complete isolation, even if only for a short period of time, made me tear up.

Master Akio stood up and exited the tent. Turning to zip it closed behind him, he said, "I see you at temple for meditation." He obviously wanted to be alone because in all the days we had been together, we'd never walked to the temple - or pretty much anywhere - by ourselves. I quickly rolled out of my cot and dug through my duffle bag for some of my, as yet, unused electronics. I found what I was looking for, quickly dressed, grabbed my backpack, and exited the tent.

I saw Master Akio walking up the beach a fair way ahead of me. I scurried over to the cooler, which had long since stopped being cool, and grabbed a couple bottles of lukewarm water. I put them in the backpack and began the trek to the temple.

The walk to the temple felt very weird and rather lonely. When I arrived, I took off my shoes and entered. Right away I could see that Master Akio had been crying. He stood up as I entered, bowed to me, and said, "Graham, I very sorry. I not know why I be bad to you."

I walked over to Master Akio and put my hand on his shoulder, "You are not acting badly. You are acting like a man whose friend is leaving only you don't want him to go. Master Akio, I don't want to go, but I need to go back for a short period of time. I promise it will only be a short period of time. I promise I will be back in 60 days or less, and I promise I will be staying longer."

"Yes, Graham. I not want you go. I not want be alone again. I afraid you not come back and I be alone all rest of life." He gave me an unusually small, tentative smile.

It was my turn to grin like a little boy. "Master Akio, I have a surprise." I took the satellite phone from the confines of my backpack. "This is a phone. With this phone you can talk with me anytime. If I am not at my home, I have an electronic device at my home called an answering machine that will take your message and then when I get home I can hear your voice."

He stared at me incredulously. "Really?" I turned the phone on. He stared at it. After I pushed the 'on' button it took the phone a few minutes to find a satellite connection and complete its startup cycle before it beeped, indicating it was ready for use. After the beep, I punched in my phone number and hit send. I leaned closer to Master Akio so he could listen. It took a few moments before I heard the familiar ring of a telephone. After the fourth ring, my answering machine kicked in. "This is Graham. I'm not here. Leave a message."

I put the phone to my mouth. "This is Graham. I am sitting in the middle of Paradise. I was just checking to see if the satellite phone is actually working. I'll see you all in a couple days." I hit the 'end' button and the phone went silent.

I smiled at Master Akio. "I will show you how the phone works and how to keep the batteries fresh with the solar charger."

He gave me a puzzled look, "Solar charger?"

"Yes. It converts the sun's rays into electricity and the electricity charges the small batteries in the phone. I just had a funny thought - when I bought the phone, I also bought a very expensive package that allows me unlimited talking time. I didn't know why the heck I was buying that when I intended to only use the phone only for this trip. I guess the Universe guided me to buy the unlimited talking package so I could keep in touch with you."

I programmed my phone number into one of the speed dial buttons and showed Master Akio how to use it. I had him practice dialing and turning the phone off and on a few times. "When we get back to camp, I will show you how to connect the solar charger to the phone."

Master Akio was smiling again. "Graham, we meditate now."

I nodded my head in agreement. Then, in a teasing tone I said, "I didn't think you were ever going to meditate. I thought you might have forgotten how."

"Old people forget things all time. You lead meditation today."

I looked at Master Akio in surprise. He nodded his head ever so slightly, indicating to me that he really was serious about wanting me to lead our morning meditation. I protested, "We've never done a meditation where one of us leads. I don't know how to."

Master Akio grinned. "Yes, that true. But today you lead."

I was not completely comfortable leading a meditation so I continued to protest. "Why do I need to do this? What's the purpose of me leading?"

"I want to know how your spirit leads you. Let spirit lead mediation and I will know. No more talk."

I could feel my body tense at my annoyance of having to lead the meditation. I hastily closed my eyes and focused my attention on my breathing. Breathe in . . . Breathe out. . . Slowly the tension began to seep out of my body and a lightness rose in my soul.

Ever so slowly, the knowing crept into my body. I opened my mouth, doing my best to talk in a soothing, measured tone, "Sitting with your back straight, I want you to feel like there is a small rope attached to the top of your head, gently tugging your head up, helping you keep your spine straight."

I felt my body relax, "Begin by taking a deep breath in through your nose. Draw the breath through the front of your body, down into the depths of your belly. Hold this breath....holding ... Now exhale by moving your breath up through your spine and exhale through your mouth. Breathe in through your nose... Focus your attention on each breath."

I felt the energy shift in Master Akio as he moved ever so slightly, sitting closer to me. I felt a gentle touch as his hand came to rest atop mine.

Suddenly everything was black, completely black. It was like a scene from a bad science fiction movie. I felt like I was looking through someone else's eyes, but all I could see was black. I could see and hear things, but there was no sensation of touch. I felt icy cold; I felt afraid.

232

Just as suddenly as the black had come, there was light. It was the light from a small candle. I was in a room but not in a familiar one. It appeared to be a typical room from one of those Japanese movies I had seen with dividing walls made of paper. A beautiful, young Japanese woman appeared in front of me, kneeling. She was wearing a beautiful silk kimono. There was a small table in front of her. I heard a divider move to my left. Another woman came in carrying a tray. This woman was familiar. Even though I had never met her, I knew her. I heard my voice in my head. *How do I know her?* Then it hit me: this was Master Akio's mother. He had described her to me perfectly.

My mind began to race. I heard my voice again. *Who the heck is this other woman? Master Akio said that before he left for the war, his mother was the last person to pour him tea. Did Master Akio lie to me?*

The beautiful, young lady took the tray from Master Akio's mother. His mother left, closing the door behind her. My voice again! *Who is this woman serving tea to Master Akio? My god, she is beautiful!*

I felt another voice in my head. Yes, she was! It sounded like Master Akio. Now I was completely freaked out. Was I in some kind of weird trance? How was this happening? Who was talking to whom, and who was in whose head? How could someone else be in my head?

Master Akio's voice spoke again. *Slow down breathing. Come back to calm spot. Focus on breath.*

I was starting to think that after almost 30 days in the tropical heat I was losing it. I was hearing voices in my head as clear as if we were talking. Was this real?

I heard Master Akio's gentle voice inside my head again. *Graham, this is real.*

I felt Master Akio's presence, then, as abruptly as it started, I was aware of my own body once again. My eyes flew open, "What was that!?"

"Reason for you to come back and reason for you to meditate while gone."

"You have my attention. That really scared the crap out of me. What was it?"

"What you think?"

"What do you mean?"

"Your words - you say what happen. Not what you see, but what you think happen," Master Akio said patiently. It was clear he would not speak again until I answered.

I paused for a few moments trying to collect my thoughts. "It was like we shared a vision, your vision."

Master Akio nodded his head in agreement. "Yes, that what happen. Not more."

"But how did you do that?"

Master Akio grinned. "Not I - we did that. You want learn this, you come back."

I groaned. "But Master Akio, this is cruel! Now that I know that this sharing of visions exists, you have to teach me!"

Master Akio held up his hand to silence me just as I started to protest. Something in his energy and body language silenced me; I sensed that I could not have spoken even if I tried.

Master Akio was quiet for a long time. Finally, he spoke, "Graham, in Japan many years I learn about KiKou. Many Chinese servants call it Qi-Gong."

My jaw dropped. "Master Akio, Sara wanted me to take a Qi-Gong class! She said I needed to learn about Qi[1]."

It was now Master Akio's turn to look utterly astonished, "You know about Qi?"

I shook my head no. "I know the word and I know it means internal energy. I've been told we can build up our Qi, but that's all I know."

Master Akio smiled, "That good. I not know how teach about Qi - bad English and you not know Japanese." Master Akio chuckled, "Universe work big mystery. You know what I worry how teach for two days!" He shook his head at the irony of the situation. "Graham, you take Qi-Gong class. You study and learn much. You need more Qi to learn what we do today. When you go home, you eat good. Eat small meals. Every day

_____

[1] Pronounced Chee, Qi is the physical life force or life energy that flows through the body

235

you meditate and exercise, stretch and run. You also take Qi-Gong lessons and journal."

"Is there anything else you would like me to do in my spare time?"

Master Akio looked at me with a very serious and stern expression. "Maybe learn fly plane better, so you not crash again, find other Master on different island."

I stared at Master Akio, waiting for his face to break into a smile. I was pretty sure he couldn't hold this serious expression long. I started a countdown. *Ten, nine, eight, seven...* His face exploded into his impish grin when I hit *six.*

"You take teasing about how you fly plane good," Master Akio said.

I pretended to be serious. "Don't say that until after I cook you breakfast."

He smiled and slowly stood up. "We go stretch."

Master Akio led us through an easy morning stretch and then sent me running towards the Dog Leg. I ran all the way there, back past the camp, and almost all the way to the temple before I could not continue. I was completely pumped. I could not remember the last time I had ever run that far. As a cool down, I walked the rest of the way to the temple and then returned to camp for breakfast.

As I entered camp, Master Akio handed me a cup of coffee. "Porridge ready soon. What you want do today, Graham? Last day together."

I thought for a few moments. "We need to make a cooler so our beer is cold tonight."

"You know how we do this?"

I smirked. "As a matter of fact, I do. It was one of the things Blaine, the Eagle Scout, taught me."

"You need Akio help?"

"Not really."

"Good! I have small project I want do. You work on cooler, I work on project."

I nodded my head in agreement but was wondering what he was up to.

After our breakfast of tinned fruit and oatmeal, we leisurely cleaned up the kitchen area, leaving the coffee and tea pots out. Since we were both working in that area, we decided we'd like a second or third cup as we worked. It seemed rather decadent to have two cups of coffee and not be rushing off to do things elsewhere on the island.

"Graham, you need saw?"

"No, the saw is all yours, but I will need the shovel."

Master Akio gave me a quick nod and walked towards the jungle. *What could he be doing that he needed to cut something in the jungle?*

I went to the supply containers and moved things around to free up two of the tubs. I planned to use one large tub, one smaller tub, and a piece of black cloth. I carried the tubs and the shovel out to our living room. I didn't want to have to walk too far for the last of the beer. I shoveled a small layer of sand into the big tub, and then placed the smaller tub on the sand inside the big tub. Next I filled the space between the two tubs with more sand.

I went back to the kitchen to put the shovel away and get a pail with a carrying handle. I used the pail to carry water from the ocean to tubs. I carefully poured the ocean water onto the sand until it was completely saturated. I had to be careful so I didn't get sand or water inside the smaller tub.

After putting the pail away, I returned to my makeshift cooler and placed the black cloth over top of the sand. I set the remaining two beers and a couple bottles of water inside the small tub. For the final step, I sealed the lid on the smaller cooler. Viola! I was done. I was rather proud of myself. I made a mental note to thank Blaine for insisting that I learn how to build this and bring the necessary supplies.

The theory of the makeshift cooler, as Blaine explained it, is that the heat of the day would heat the black cloth causing the water in the sand underneath to evaporate. The evaporation would then cool the inside container. *I really hope this works. I hate warm beer!*

I looked up as I heard Master Akio return from the jungle. He was carrying coconuts. Now he really had me curious. What was he up to?

Master Akio was grinning, "Want to help?" and before I could say anything he quickly added, "But no ask questions until I say."

Since curiosity had the best of me, I agreed to his terms.

"Good! Use saw to cut one inch long strip from middle of coconut."

Despite the fact that there were so many coconuts on the island this was the first time we had really done anything with them, besides the salad dressing and Master Akio's bowls. I decided I would have to do a little research on coconuts when I got home.

We began by ripping off the outer husk, revealing the hard coconut I was used to seeing at the grocery store. Master Akio said, "Graham, start at top of coconut and let out coconut water." It's a good thing he told me to do this or I would have had a very sticky mess.

Master Akio asked me to make six strips; three complete coconut rings cut into two halves to make them into strips. A person skilled with a saw would have only needed three coconuts to complete the task. I needed five coconuts to get the required number of strips in the right dimensions – the saw and I were not exactly on friendly terms.

Master Akio came over and inspected my work, "Very good, Graham. Now use knife to make small hole in coconut strips. Like I show you when we make swords."

"One hole for each strip?"

Master Akio appeared to be thinking. "No. Two holes - one at each end."

I went to the cutlery container to find the hunting knife. Once found, I returned to my coconuts. I heard Master Akio start a fire.

I had the second hole on one of the strips completed when Master Akio returned, sliding my lukewarm coffee under my nose. "Graham, take break. Project to be fun and relaxing! I sorry not say sooner."

I took a sip of my coffee and decided it was still okay to drink. I chuckled, "So, are you really not going to tell me what we are making?"

He shook his head. "No tell what making, but tell you work with love."

I set my coffee down and looked at Master Akio, "Is that not the way you have asked me to do things, all things, ever since we built the temple?"

"Yes." He winked and added, "Need more love in this."

I finished my coffee and picked up the knife to continue drilling the small holes in the remaining five strips. I took my time drilling the others, stopping frequently to refill my coffee or Master Akio's tea.

When I had completed all the holes, Master Akio came over and inspected my work. "Very good, Graham." He took a small piece of paper from his pocket and began to unfold it. "Graham, this paper have Japanese writing called Kanji. This

Kanji mean something very special." He raised his hand to silence me before I had a chance to ask any questions. "I tell you at fire tonight what it means. For now, know this Kanji very special, very powerful."

He grinned and continued, "Graham, you have more fun today! I teach you to write these two Kanji." He pointed to the paper he'd unfolded.

I looked at the complete mess of lines on the page and stared incredulously at Master Akio, "Are you serious?"

"Yes, I bring paper from Old Home to practice. You have pen. Please go get pen and we start." Master Akio must have seen the look of disbelief on my face as I got up to go to the tent. He called out, "You do good, Graham. I teach you."

The heat inside the tent was almost unbearable. If it was 100°F outside, it felt like it was 140°F inside. I quickly grabbed my journal, the ink bottle, and pen before hastily retreating. I made a side trip over to my makeshift cooler on the way back to the table. I popped the lid off and grabbed what I hoped would be a cool bottle of water. Eureka! It was cool. Not cold, but cool none the less. I grabbed a bottle of water for Master Akio and quickly put the lid back on. I returned to the kitchen and presented the bottle of water to Master Akio. He took it from me and said, "Cooler works good! Thank you, Graham."

We both took long, refreshing swigs before starting our next task. Master Akio's began teaching me the art of Kanji.

First he taught me the 'Rules':

241

1. Top to bottom
2. Left to right
3. Center strokes are written before wings
4. Center strokes connecting to other strokes are written first
5. Center strokes passing through other strokes are written last
6. Frames that enclose other strokes are written first, but closed last
7. Right-to-left diagonals are written before left-to-right diagonals

My head was swimming with all the rules. Master Akio smiled, "I show you. I use your pen?"

I handed my pen to Master Akio. He opened the bottle, and dipped the end in the ink. He drew the first character on the paper three times. On the third time he got me to number the strokes as he created the Kanji character so I would know the order that they went in.

Master Akio handed me back the pen and, for what seemed like hours, I practiced writing the one Kanji character. He interrupted me numerous times with various words of encouragement. "Yes, very good." "No, wrong order." "Yes, very nice." At last, he finally said, "Very good Graham. Now I show you other character."

I groaned loudly. Master Akio grinned, "No worry, Graham. I teach you hard character first. Next character easy."

"Easy for who?"

"Easy for you." He took the pen and made a lopsided happy face with a line on the right side.

I looked up at him, "That's it?"

Master Akio grinned. "Yes! See! I save easy one for last."

I took the pen from Master Akio and tried writing out the character I had just seen without any further instruction. He gave his proud grin; I had done well. He put his hand on my shoulder, "Strokes correct, but wrong order. Follow only left to right."

So I tried writing the character again. Master Akio smiled, "Perfect. Now write this character first. Write other one on top, like this." He took the pen from me and wrote the characters vertically, one stacked on top of the other. I was amazed at the sheer grace of his hand and how fluid his writing was. The pen moved like an extension of his hand, not a separate tool.

Master Akio looked at the paper and then at me. "Now you do this." He handed me back the pen. I took the pen and practiced for what seemed like eternity. Master Akio continually interrupted, "Good! Now make it smaller." My characters went from three inches high each to both characters sitting inside a space no bigger than one inch wide by two and a half inches tall.

Finally, Master Akio said, "Graham, stop. You are good Kanji student. You learn good. You learn two characters in one day. Very good. Now we take small break. Then we finish project. You want tea or coffee?"

I slowly moved from the kitchen. I had been standing for a long time and my body was sore. "I'd like coffee please. After tomorrow, I won't have anyone to make me coffee for a while."

Master Akio walked to the stove. "Maybe if you nice to Sara she make you coffee. I think you have to be nice."

I could tell by his tone that he was teasing and testing me. I grinned, "I can be nice. How's this? Sara, get me coffee, you lazy bum!"

"Oh, Graham. Words like that! Sara pour you coffee - pour coffee on you!"

"I think you're right. I think I might have to be extra nice."

Master Akio nodded in agreement. "I only make you three more coffee, Graham. We have coffee now, supper, and breakfast. Then no more coffee. You need bring more coffee when you come back."

"More coffee it is."

Master Akio brought my coffee to me. "Graham, for project we heat metal and burn character in coconut strip. I not know how this work. Kanji on paper easy. Kanji on coconut...I not do this before. See Father do this, but I not do this."

I was confused. "What are we going to use to burn the Kanji into the coconut?"

Master Akio walked over to the fire that I hadn't even seen him light because I'd been so engrossed in my Kanji work. He picked up a small object, and brought it over for me to look at. It looked like a spoon handle. The bowl of the spoon had been broken off and the handle was embedded in a piece of wood.

"Oh my, this will be exciting. I just learned to write two characters with a pen and now you want me to write out the same characters using this large tool?"

"Yes. We not learn until we try new things. We have coconut shells to practice on first. When good, we do on strips with hole."

I rolled my eyes in disbelief.

"Graham, you come to island. You think you meet Japanese man? Learn to meditate or sword fight? Build temple? Learn to fish?"

I could only reply with a sheepish, "No."

"Graham, you not do before. Not mean you not do now. Graham, you only believe what you see. Learn to believe first and then you see."

"I think I understand, but I have 42 years of bad habits to undo."

"That okay. Tokyo not build in one day."

I burst into laughter. Master Akio looked at me like I was possessed, "What I say?"

I tried three or four times to talk but couldn't stop the laughter. Soon, Master Akio was laughing with me. I guess my laughter was contagious.

Gradually, I regained control and was able to say, "I thought it was funny because you haven't seen people in over 60 years, yet somehow you used a saying similar to one that I know. I know it as 'Rome wasn't built in a day'."

Master Akio grinned. "Hmmm, maybe Japanese take from Romans. I think wise words last long time." I nodded in agreement.

"We try finish project." Master Akio picked up the shovel, went to the fire and scooped some warm embers. He carried them to the kitchen and poured some of them into an empty chicken flakes can. The can had a notch in it, which I assume was to hold our scribing tool. He handed me the shovel that still had a few hot embers on it and asked me to take it all back to the fire and throw another log on. I went to complete my tasks.

I returned to find the scribing tool lying across the can as I suspected and Master Akio gently blowing on the embers. He looked up at me and explained, "Keep hot," and then returned to blowing softly. It didn't take long for the end of the scribing tool to become red hot.

Carefully, Master Akio picked it up and started to scribe on a random piece of trash coconut shell. Smoke rose from the coconut. Master Akio continued scribing for only a short period of time before returning the tool to the holder for reheating. When it was hot again, he continued on with the scribing process. He repeated the whole process on three or four more scraps of coconut shell before he decided to try it on one of the 'good' strips.

I handed Master Akio a good piece of coconut - one of the pieces with the holes drilled in it. He lifted the hot scribing tool and began to write. He returned the tool to the heat only four or five times before he placed the tool down and showed me his work. It looked pretty darn good. The colour was pretty even all the way through.

Master Akio turned to me, "You do now." Hesitantly, I began to blow on the embers as he had done. When the scribing tip was red hot I carefully picked it up. Master Akio handed me a scrap piece of coconut.

I saw and felt the tip of the scribing tool sear the coconut shell. I slid the tool along the strip, scribing the first character. It was a bit bulkier than the pen but the tool slid across the coconut shell with only a little resistance. I was genuinely surprised at how easily it worked.

I practiced on six more pieces before I felt confident enough to work on one of the prepared pieces. I looked at Master Akio. "Okay, I'm ready. Can you hand me a good strip of coconut?"

He smiled and said, "Very good," as he handed me the requested strip. I took my time and carefully wrote the two characters. I put the tool down inside the holder and looked at my completed work of art. A huge grin crept across my face. It looked pretty good!

After I inspected it, I handed it to Master Akio. He carefully looked it over. "Very good work." He handed it back to me, "Now, please make two more."

"Two more?" I exclaimed in surprise

Master Akio picked up the saw and simply said, "Yes, two more please."

By the time I completed the two other pieces and dumped the embers back into the fire, Master Akio had cut down all the completed pieces with the saw. They were now all about one inch wide and two and a half inches tall with a hole on the top of the long side. As he was inspecting all the finished pieces one more time, I walked over and stood next to my Master. "So, what's next?"

He looked up to the sky. "Soon it rain. We clean up, burn practice papers, put your journal and pen in tent, then go fishing."

"I would love to do some fishing."

I had just closed the tent after returning my journaling materials to their proper place when the sky opened up and literally dumped rain down on me. I was completely soaked before I could run the 30 feet from the tent to the safety of the kitchen awning. At least the rain was warm. Since I was already wet, I walked over to the container with the fishing gear, opened the lids, took out the spear gun and the mask, and started toward the ocean. I called back to Master Akio, "Coming?"

"Yes."

It felt like we spent the entire afternoon swimming, fishing, and playing in the waves, when it was only a couple of hours. Yet, for those few precious hours, I felt like a child again. I felt truly alive. It was magical and transformational. I was living the childhood I never had. I was frolicking in the water on a beach with a man who was more like a dad to me than my own father.

The old Graham wanted to be sad and bitter; after all, this was the childhood he so desperately wanted and needed. The new Graham only wanted to rejoice in the sheer joy of the experience and live the moment to its fullest.

Hunger and exhaustion finally drove us from the water to the kitchen for a supper of fish, rice, and tinned green beans. The atmosphere was celebratory. We both knew tomorrow was going to be hard, so we were reveling in each other's company right now; we were having fun.

As usual, I carried Master Akio's food to his chair before getting my own. I made a third and final trip to get our tea and coffee. Master Akio was already sitting when I returned with his tea. As always, he graciously accepted with a, "Thank you, Graham."

"You're welcome."

Today we timed our meal perfectly. As I sat down, the sun began to sink into the distant horizon. I was amazed by the variety of hues of reds and oranges. The colors seemed more vibrant than any other sunset we'd seen so far. It felt like this sunset was the most spectacular, as if the Universe was giving us some form of good-bye present. We both sat and watched the sun set in silence. There were no words adequate for the moment.

After we washed the dishes and cleaned up the kitchen, we took coffee and tea back to the living room. We piled wood on the fire until it was a huge, roaring bon-fire.

Master Akio stood and faced me, "Graham, you do very special work today. I surprise what you know. I ask you question now - you know what Dao[2] is?"

I looked at him and replied, "I think so. It is a spiritual belief. It's a way of behaving."

"Ok, that work. Graham, Dao also called 'The Way'. Today you make Kanji characters. One is Dao. Other is Shin – it mean heart. But not just heart in body. It is spirit heart. Today you write Shin Dao –The Dao of Heart or Way of Heart. Graham, everything you learn here on island about heart."

He smiled gently at me, "I see you learn to love more. Graham not so angry at world. Find peace in self. You say today, everything we do - make food, build temple - we do with love. Graham, please stand here." He pointed to a spot directly in front of him. I got up and walked over to stand in front of him.

---

[2] Pronounced Dow, Dao is frequently spelled with a T instead of a D.

"Graham, you and Universe give me task to be Master. I think many days on what I teach and what I want you teach others. I meditate many days on this." He reached into his pocket and pulled out one of the scribed coconut strips. There was now a string attached to the shell.

I felt an energy shift in Master Akio as tears appeared at the corners of his eyes. "Graham, I ask many times what purpose in life is, why I come to this island. I ask why Akio have no children, what Universe want Akio do. Graham, when you say yes, you be student and I be master, I know all I learn be for this."

Tears were now freely streaming down Master Akio's face. "Graham, Shin Dao is way of life. When you live Shin Dao you live all moments. Graham, this coconut make you remember all things Shin Dao. It make you remember live from heart. Graham, you take Shin Dao coconut? You say yes to live Shin Dao – our path?"

As he called it 'our path,' a huge lump formed in my throat and tears gently rolled down my face. I had never been in a club, fraternity, gang, or even taken part in a Hollywood style handshake and spit pact. To be symbolically bound together with someone was truly overwhelming for me.

I was unable to speak, so I just nodded, accepting Master Akio's gift. He smiled through his tears and slipped the necklace over my head. Because of my childhood, I was never a hugging person, but after the necklace was slipped around my

251

head, I found myself being drawn to give Master Akio a hug. I threw my arms around him and drew him in for a massive bear hug.

After a long, heartfelt embrace, Master Akio stepped back and took another necklace out of his pocket, "Graham, you make this coconut strip with Kanji. I like wear this, if ok? You have Kanji I make."

Master Akio's question took me a little bit by surprise. "Of course you can wear it! Actually, I would be honoured if you wore it."

I reached over and gently took it from his hand. I clasped the string between both of my hands and stepped back to gather my thoughts. The huge lump in my throat returned. I stepped forward, "I didn't really know I had a heart until I met you. You showed me glimpses of who I really can become." I was unable to speak or even swallow as the lump continued to grow. Tears began streaming down my face again. I had cried more in the last 30 days than I had cried in my 42 years of life.

I looked Master Akio directly in the eyes. I started to open my mouth to speak, but was unable to. I breathed deeply and tried again. The words came out slowly and as a whispery rasp, "Master Akio, you showed me how to love myself and for that I am eternally grateful. You showed me what a real father could be like. You showed me what living the Shin Dao really means. For that and more, I thank you."

252

Tears streamed down Master Akio's face. I did my best to remember what he had said to me as he offered me the gift, "Master Akio, this necklace is a reminder of all things sacred. It is a reminder to live Shin Dao – the Way of the Heart. It is a reminder for you to stay true to your heart. As my Master of the Shin Dao, will you accept this necklace as a symbol of our path?"

When he nodded, I placed the sacred necklace over his head. He stepped forward and gave me a warm, heartfelt hug. For a moment my minded drifted to Blaine. *I better not tell Blaine about all this hugging or I'll never live it down!* I was always making fun of him for hugging his dad. I smiled. I think I was slowly starting to understand my friend.

Master Akio gradually stepped back and pulled the other two necklaces out of his pocket. He held them out to me and said, "These for your friends, Sara and Blaine. You choose how to give them."

I furrowed my brow. "Why am I giving Sara and Blaine one?"

Master Akio smiled, "Because Sara and Blaine your friends. How else we teach world about Shin Dao, if not share? Put in pocket. Now we have beer."

I was going to protest a little bit more but Master Akio spoke the magic word, 'beer.' So, I carefully pocketed the necklaces and went to the make-shift cooler.

Master Akio added a few more logs to the fire; perhaps all the logs. In anticipation of the size of the flames, Master Akio moved his chair further back from the fire pit. I set down the two beers and walked over to my bench to take it apart so we could move it back, as well. We didn't quite get it together perfectly though, so it was pretty wobbly. Master Akio said, "Only need tonight and breakfast. No worry!"

He sat in his chair and I cautiously lowered myself down onto my wobbly bench. The fire was already burning rather hot, even though only about a third of the wood was actually burning. *I think we might be moving back even further.* Within a few minutes we were forced back by the heat. This time we moved a fair distance away.

After rebuilding my bench - again - we settled in and silently gazed into the blazing fire. After a while I broke our trance-like state by reaching over and handing Master Akio his beer. He silently took it from me, nodding his head in thanks. Almost in unison, we twisted the bottle caps off and turned to face the ocean, raising our bottles in salute. To complete our ritual, we turned and faced each other, clinked our glass beer bottles together, said, "Cheers", and finally took deep, slow swallows of our perfectly chilled beer. We both ended our long, leisurely drink with a lip smacking, "Ahhhhhh!" We lowered our bottles to our sides and returned our gaze to the now gigantic bon-fire.

We repeated our beer drinking ceremony half a dozen more times before the last drop of the pale elixir was drained from our bottles. *One more beer would have been perfect, but it's a long swim to get one.* I returned my gaze to the fire.

Suddenly, I felt a big energy shift in Master Akio. I turned my head and faced him, curious as to what was up. He inhaled a deep breath and then in a low tone began to chant what sounded like, "Who. . . Shoe. . . Foo. . . Way. . . Chemmy. . . She. . ." He continued to chant for a few minutes, setting a tone and rhythm. Then, without missing so much as a beat, he invited me, "Graham, you also."

I felt really awkward as I joined in, since I was continually stumbling over the words, "Who. . . Shoe. . . Foo. . . Way. . . Chemmy. . . She. . ." I soon got the hang of it and no longer stumbled over the words, or the order. It didn't take long before I felt the chants begin to resonate deep within my body. I began to relax.

We chanted together for a very, very long time. I don't know how I knew, but I sensed the exact moment that Master Akio was going to stop and we stopped in perfect unison. Our roaring bon-fire had burned down to just a small pile of embers. I felt peaceful and fully alive. It was a phenomenal sensation. My whole body tingled with energy.

Master Akio stood up slowly. "Graham, that healing chant. You can teach to Sara and Blaine. Tomorrow is busy day. I go to bed. Good night, friend."

Even though I was energized and buzzed, I stood up and followed Master Akio. "You are correct. Tomorrow is going to be a long day."

Day Thirty – Going Home

Once again, I felt the morning heat building in the tent. As I rolled over to greet Master Akio with a cheerful, "Good morning," my newly acquired spider senses kicked in completely. Danger, Graham, danger! Without thinking, I threw my arm up to protect my face. Somehow Master Akio had taken my pillow and was in the midst of swinging it at my head. In a pillow fight, nothing is worse than getting pummeled with your own pillow.

I deflected the first, second, and barely managed to protect myself from the third blow, but I was physically unable to deflect the forth. I was completely vulnerable as I was doubled over, hysterically laughing at Master Akio. His look of childish glee was just too much for me; my dignified master wailing on me with a pillow was too funny.

After the second blow to my unprotected body, Master Akio abruptly stopped and smiled at me. "I want do that for many days. Today perfect day to do that. Thank you!" He dropped the pillow to the floor and said, "We go meditate. It very hot in here."

Still laughing at the memory of Master Akio attacking me with the pillow, I quickly changed into shorts and a new t-shirt so that I, too, could flee the rapidly rising heat of the tent.

I flopped down on my bench. Master Akio was still smiling, "That fun!" He paused and then complimented me, "You sense much better."

"Thank you!"

"You talk all morning or we meditate?" he asked sarcastically.

"Hey, it was you that started this!" I followed up with a fake pout. We both chuckled at our morning follies.

We were still smiling like Cheshire cats as we tried to settle into our meditations. I closed my eyes and began to focus on my breathing. A thought flashed through my mind to gently punch Master Akio in the arm. I didn't even have time to act when he said, "I not do that if I you!"

My eyes flew open and I swung my head around like a possessed man. I stared directly at Master Akio. "How did you do that?"

Master Akio smiled and shrugged his shoulders, "Same way you know I hit you with pillow."

I guess if I understood how I'd known that he was going to hit me with a pillow, I might have been more satisfied with his answer. Since I didn't, all I could do was slowly turn around and face towards the ocean again. I didn't like the answer, but I knew he was not going to give me any more than he already had. Rather than being frustrated, I chose to settle into a comfortable position, close my eyes, and concentrate on my breathing.

We meditated for a long while before I felt Master Akio stir. I still had my eyes closed when he spoke, "I think we still have oats and fruit for breakfast. Graham, today no run."

I wasn't really all that surprised. I had a lot of things to do this morning, like pack up my whole camp. Slowly, I opened my eyes and gazed out at the ocean. I was struck by the notion that I would really miss this place. I stood up and quietly followed Master Akio into the kitchen. It seemed rather odd to have us both preparing breakfast. We were used to our routine.

Master Akio prepared the oatmeal and I made our hot beverages. I took Master Akio's oatmeal and tea to his chair, then collected my own food and drink. I sat down beside him and we both ate quietly while staring out to the vast expanse of the sparkling, blue ocean.

I gathered all our breakfast dishes and cleaned up. It didn't take long before the dishes were done and everything was put away. Master Akio did not remove his eyes from the ocean. He let out a heavy sigh, "It is time to clean up, Graham."

I nodded in agreement and went to the tent, aka our sauna, to pack everything inside it before the heat was unbearable. I worked quickly in the sweltering heat. Once it was empty, I took the tent down and neatly stacked it and all its contents in the kitchen.

In the meantime, Master Akio dug a big hole a fair walk up the beach, down near the low tide mark, and buried all the hot ashes. He also covered up the fire- pit with fresh sand, leaving no trace.

I folded down the kitchen table, packed all the remaining gear, including the stove, into the appropriate storage containers. The only thing left to do was take down the kitchen awning. I took half a dozen steps back and looked at my old adversary. How I dreaded, then hated, putting it up. Now, I hated taking it down. The physical task was no longer the problem; it signified the end - the end of an excellent adventure. Who could have ever thought my stay on the island would turn out as it did?

I walked towards the kitchen then easily and quickly shinnied up each of the trees that were holding the awning. As I slid down the last one, jumping the last few feet to the ground, I remembered the feeling of the exhaustion when I first put up the awning. I vividly remembered how my whole body ached. Now, 28 days later, climbing the trees was almost effortless. It was amazing how much I had changed in only a month.

Together, we folded the awning and stacked it neatly with the other gear.

Master Akio graciously filled the hole we'd dug in the jungle that served as our toilet. When he returned with the shovel, I offered him a small bow, a nod of my head, and an enthusiastic, "Thank you!"

He bowed back and smiled, "You bow much better than first day I meet you!"

I grinned. "Oh, yes and I feel much better, too."

Master Akio became serious "We walk to Dog Leg."

I let out a sigh. We both turned and began the slow, dreaded trek to the Dog Leg, knowing that when we reached it, it would mean good-bye. That way neither of us had to watch the other walk away.

Part-way to the Dog Leg, Master Akio asked, "Please take many pictures of your friend, Sara. I like to see and know more about her. Take many pictures of things you hold sacred. Bring pictures back with you."

I replied, "I will do that. I will take lots of pictures for you."

"Thank you."

Unfortunately, it didn't take us long to arrive at the Dog Leg. If there was ever a moment in my life to dread, this was it. How do you say good-bye to someone who has just taught you to say hello to life? I could feel the tears well up in my eyes.

Master Akio and I faced each other. I smiled. He smiled. "When good-bye hard, we know we alive; we feel from our hearts. Graham, I feel so much from heart now, I think it burst!" Tears started to pour down Master Akio's face. He looked me straight in the eye. "Graham, you come back. Not let old man die on island alone."

With that, I also burst into tears. I fiercely grabbed Master Akio in a hug; my heart breaking. I sobbed, "I will be back. I promise you, Master Akio, I will be back."

I felt him grip me tightly. "You are good friend, Graham."

"Master Akio, I love you very much. You take care of yourself."

I had no idea where that came from, but I spoke the words of my soul heart. I felt Master Akio squeeze me tighter. I had never before cried because someone was leaving and I didn't like the feeling. To care for someone so much that leaving them felt like it was tearing apart my soul was actually painful.

We stood there, locked in a big hug, frozen in time. Neither of us wanted this to end, yet we knew that separation was inevitable. I think I had a glimmer of what a mother must go through on the first day that she sends her child to school. Rationally, I knew that I would be back in 60 days or less, but that didn't make saying good-bye any easier.

I felt the energy in Master Akio change. Little by little, he gradually let go of me until his hands finally dropped to his sides. Taking a few steps back, he came to attention. He bowed a deep, fluid and graceful bow, held it for a moment before elegantly rising and coming back to attention. He stood there, his eyes locked onto mine, tears still flowing unabashedly down his face.

I came to attention. With the knowing that everything and everyone is sacred, and with all the care and love I had for my Master, friend, and surrogate father, I bowed. It was my best bow ever. I held it for a moment and then I rose. I locked eyes with Master Akio and stood at attention.

"Graham, if I had son, I wish it be you. I love you, my friend." He held my tear soaked gaze for a moment, then turned and walked towards his home. I was filled with grief as he turned. I watched for a few seconds, not really wanting him to leave, but each step he took away from me was more painful to watch. When I could bear it no more, I turned and walked towards my camp.

I had walked only part-way back when I was filled with the knowledge that the boat would be here soon.

I had been home almost two weeks; the days seemed to blur together. I was finally able to get around to unpacking my duffle bag of clothes. I undid the top buckle and with a sigh, simply turned the bag over and dumped the contents on the floor.

Clothes fell everywhere. I collapsed onto my knees and burst into tears. On the floor before me lay a tiny, tattered and thread-bare brown uniform mixed within my clothes. I gently picked it up; it even smelled like Master Akio. I missed my friend terribly.

*"Your years of training and
practice have prepared you for
this moment.
Breathe . . .
Step Forward . . .
In each moment the miracle of
you will unfold. . .
Allow."*

-Akio

A Warriors Heart: Perseverance
June 25, 2014 Release Date

The Four Pillars of the Shin Dao

Opening Hearts

Inspiring Minds

Developing Bodies

Elevating Spirits

"There is a magnet in your heart that will attract true friends. That magnet is unselfishness, thinking of others first... when you learn to live for others, they will live for you."

- Paramahansa Yogananda

www.shindao.com

Order your own Shin Dao Amulet at www.amulet.shindao.com

Made in the USA
Charleston, SC
07 September 2014